Olivia's Prison

LOVE AND VAMPIRES
BOOK TWO

RHIANNON FUTCH

For anyone in their own personal prison,
I hope you find your freedom
And all the happiness.

Contents

Chapter One

Olivia

I don't know what to wear to a trial like this. Should I dress to impress? Maybe I should ask Roman? I think I should because, honestly, I'd like to go tell the lot of them off. Unfortunately, Duncan keeps telling me that isn't an option, and there are worse things than death. Nims shoves her head into my hand, and I scratch automatically. We aren't usually apart during stressful things, and the fact that I can't take her with me stresses us both.

"Come on, let's go ask Roman what I should wear to this utter bullshit of a trial." She stands and leads the way out of the closet. This place that Roman calls home is a maze of rooms and hallways. Filled as it is with the spoils of war and conquest, I have been at him since I first saw the place to give it all back.

I may be starting to win. It seems like pieces are going missing around here. Coming down the stairs, I would swear there are two more paintings gone. I can hear Roman telling someone to figure things out. I wonder what presses their attention so. His office door is open, so we walk in and wait.

He tells the man he is talking to, "Go. See that you do it right this time." After the man leaves, he sits down and looks at me. "How are you and Nims this evening?"

Nims leans into my leg, and I set my hand on her head, petting her. "Nervous. I don't know what to expect, and I am scared about the whole thing. I don't know what to wear. I don't want to leave Nims here, while I go to this trial about who I live with, especially when it shouldn't be a thing at all. I am well-past being grown. I don't like it. So, what should I wear?"

He nods and steeples his hands in front of his chest, elbows resting on the arms of his chair. "You should go for elegance and business. If you have a suit of some sort, that would be ideal. As for the rest, would you shut the door, please?" I shut the door without fuss because he actually asked and said please. For once. "Thank you. I don't blame you for being nervous. Honestly, it is strange that this trial is even being entertained. I hear rumblings of things that give me pause. I have concerns that this may have been decided already and not in our favor."

My heart freezes in my chest. "What do you mean, 'it may have been decided' like that? They can't do that, right? Do we have a backup plan? What happens to Nims?"

I kneel next to her and hug her hard. She leans into me, laying her head over my shoulder. Roman stands and comes over. He kneels in front of us, putting a hand on my shoulder. "We will keep her safe. If the worst happens, and you must go with Callum, we will keep her safe. I swear it."

I can feel tears running down my face. I may not blush anymore, but I can cry rivers of blood. Roman pats my back about as awkwardly as possible. "What will you do, when she and I can't take being apart? We've never been apart for more than some hours. I don't know what I would do without her."

"You'll send us dirty clothing, so she can have your scent near her. Ultimately, we will find some way for you to see her regularly. We will keep fighting to have you brought back here and to adopt you. It is the only way to keep you and us safe. Callum is only interested in owning you. He hasn't any idea about the people, the church, that is after you. I think he will tire of you. Well, after he finds out you aren't willing to fall at his feet and worship him."

"Well, you've met me. The only creature I might worship is my Nims. I'll hate Callum, if he takes me from her." Straightening, I look at Roman. "I'll make him regret ever having seen me for taking me from her."

Roman says, "Good. Do it within the confines of polite society. Vampires are long lived, and we have created a ridiculous amount of rules. One such being that you can't kill your sire for pissing you off."

"What's the use of being a vampire, if I can't kill any and all people for pissing me off?" I huff.

Roman chuckles and pulls out a red handkerchief as he says, "I agree with you, but this is the world we live in. I suppose, if you don't like it, you could campaign and become the high ruler of the council. If you are that determined."

His words spark something in me. Taking the handkerchief, I wipe the tears from my face. "Is that really a possibility? Anyone can do that?"

He nods and stands, moving back to his desk. "Yes, anyone. Even a rogue. The reason most vampires do not is because of the difficulty involved. Vampires tend to hate change. They want things to be the same all the time because it makes time seem to stand still for them. The passing centuries seem shorter and less frequent. The older vampires especially feel such urges. The resistance to change is fierce.

They do not want anyone young coming in and fucking up their cozy, insular lives."

"Maybe that is what they need." Shoving the soiled handkerchief in my pocket, I stand. "Perhaps I will become high ruler of the council, if this goes wrong. Maybe I will, so I can burn it all to the ground. I'll dress for this bullshit in the meantime."

It seems like only a second had passed when Duncan knocks on my door and opens it. "Are you ready to go?"

Pressing one more kiss to the top of Nims' head, I stand. "Stay here, my sweet girl. I'll be back soon. Hopefully, with good news."

Nims nods at me, and I join Duncan in the hall. He takes my arm in his as we head for the front door. Roman and Niall waited next to a car. The driver sits in the car, waiting for us all to climb in. Niall opens the car door when we come out, and Roman joins us. We follow Niall, who gets in last and closes the door behind him. The driver takes off, and my nerves ramp up another notch as we approach my doom. Everyone is silent, lost in their thoughts. The one eddy of swirling upset I can't escape is what will I do without my Nims? She is my rock, my best friend. We have each other's backs in ways I wouldn't trust anyone else.

I would miss Blair and Duncan, but they can't compare to my Nims.

If I could still sweat, my palms would be soaked as we glide to a smooth stop in front of a squat, dark building that looks more like a warehouse. Two men come out to greet us as we unfold out of the car. By greet, I mean watch us until we near the doors. Roman puts his arms up, and one of the men pats him down. Niall is next, and the man smiles a little as his hands move toward me. Instead of patting, his hands start to slide down my body, until they jerk away violently. The other man rushes over as I turn to find Duncan crushing the man's hands for an improper pat down.

"Your manners are poor, friend. I don't know what made you think it would be a good idea to grope Olivia in front of her family." The sound of the bones cracking in the man's hands sends a shiver down my spine. "We aren't going to allow it. I'm going to let you off with a warning this time, but you should learn some manners before it becomes detrimental to your health." He releases the man's hands. They are mangled and horrific to look at. I think I'll put that in a book. The other man had stopped, standing next to me. He shrugs and says, "Very well, I will continue the pre-entry checks. Bran, sit next to the doors until your hands heal. However, Olivia, I need to recheck you."

I nod and he pats me down, impersonally and quickly, before he moves on to Duncan.

We go inside without further incident, and another man waits to lead us down a hall to a room. He opens the door and motions for us to enter. The lighting is dim, but plenty enough for vampires. Callum stands off to the right of the door, just inside the jam itself. Roman leads us off to the left. The far side of the room is so dark, all that we can see is the barest outline of a long table and some people sitting behind it. So much for vampiric vision. Roman turns and touches my elbow, guiding me to stand next to him.

As I stop next to him, the lights dangling over the people across the room turn on. The lights reveal hooded figures cloaked in mystery and darkness. I feel anxiety in the pit of my stomach as Roman's words from earlier run through my mind on repeat. I dart a glance at Callum to find him watching me. His face is a mask, no emotion visible.

Someone at the table speaks. I can't tell who, as the voice

doesn't seem to come from any one place. "Callum, explain why you have petitioned us."

Callum's attention turns to them as he tells the story of what happened when he turned me. He was attacked that night, too. No wonder he never came back. He had no recollection of me until he saw my picture on the back of one of my books. Of course. Note to self, no more pictures there or maybe anywhere. That shit just causes problems. The room is silent as he tells them his story and ends with saying, "We were both robbed of the time we should have had to train her and to come to know each other. Admittedly, I broke rules in choosing to turn her, but she would have died, if I had not. I thought if she hated it, and I couldn't convince her otherwise, then I would return her to death."

The voice speaks again. "Very well. Olivia will spend one year learning from Callum Mezzasalma and familiarizing herself with the family she was reborn into. At that time, the court will revisit this matter. Adjourned."

My jaw drops, and I move to step forward and speak, but I am snatched back. Roman moves to stand in front of me as Duncan holds me against him, his hand pressed over my mouth. Roman thanks them for their time, and we all leave the room. Callum follows behind us. I can feel his eyes on me. We go outside and Duncan releases me. I straighten my clothing and smooth my hair. Callum waits till I look up to say, "I would like for you to be ready to leave two nights from now."

"And I would like for you to take a long walk off a short pier. What the fuck are you doing? I don't want to go with you. How does your pea brain decide that forcing me to go with you is the way to get me to accept you all as family?"

Callum starts to speak, but Duncan's fist lands before he gets a word out. Callum licks the blood from his lip and smiles. "You have one because I will be taking her home with me." Duncan moves to hit him again, and Callum blocks it. "I understand you two have a thing. Don't worry, I'll bring her back, eventually. She might even remember your name by then."

Roman puts a hand on Duncan's shoulder. Duncan looks at Callum and puts his fist down. Roman studies Callum, then he says, "Callum, she will be ready in three days. You may leave with her on the evening of the third day. She will need the full, two days to sort her affairs."

Callum nods with his eyes wondering over my face and a smile. "I accept. See you then, sweetheart."

"Eat a dick, asshole."

Chapter Two

Duncan

Roman was right. The courts have been bought. All the safeguards put in place, all the things the vampire community did to ensure this court remained impartial, they were all to no avail. The court is corrupted nonetheless. Callum's fucking face pisses me off. He always looks so smug. It just makes me want to see if he still looks so condescending after he swallows his teeth. Getting in the car and away from the desire to test the theory was a relief. Until Olivia starts to cry next to me, dammit. I put my arms around her and hold her close. "It won't be so bad as it seems. Callum is an asshole, but he isn't always like that. It seems like he honestly meant to take care of you and was trying to save your life."

She sniffles and lifts her head. In a voice raw with pain, she says, "I don't give a fuck about Callum. I don't care about having to go there. I care about Nims! I can't risk taking her there. What if they figure out what she is? I can't risk her life, and I don't know if I can handle being separated from her."

"I'll take care of her. I'll take care of the rest of your dogs, even, while you are there. We'll video chat daily, so you can see her. We'll find ways to keep you in contact as much as possible. I mean, we can probably get the witches in on this. A year will pass so quick, and you'll be reunited with her. I promise."

She cries harder, and I know she isn't buying any of what I said. I can't even blame her. I've never seen any two people as close as her and that dog. The car pulls up to the front doors of Roman's place. The engine has barely stopped when Olivia is out and running into the house. I know exactly where I'll find her. As we climb out of the vehicle, we can hear Nims howling. Poor dog. Poor Olivia. Callum is doing himself no favors by taking her from this place. One of the other enforcers steps up as Niall gets out of the car behind Roman. "Sir, there's something I think you should know."

Roman's hand comes up to pinch the bridge of his own nose. "What now?"

The enforcer says, "Olivia's house burned to the ground while you all were in court. However, there's more."

"Oh, fucking hell. Spit it out, man."

"They painted red crosses on what remains of the fence, and they planted huge, metal crosses in the front yard."

"Fuck. I know Olivia doesn't want to go with Callum, but it might be for the best, if she is gone for a little while. It might confuse these bastards and throw them off her trail. I think we should keep this to ourselves for a bit. She is upset already, and I don't want to give her a reason to shed more tears."

CALLUM

One more day of pacing this fucking hotel might actually drive me insane. In less than twelve hours, hopefully she will leave with me. Unless she took this time as an opportunity to run from me because she really does find me abhorrent.

Somehow, I don't think my presence is the problem beyond fucking up plans, and that is mostly because Roman had plans to add her to his family. Even that doesn't ring true. Something else holds her here. I want to know. No, I need to know what it is that had her so upset about leaving that she was willing to risk the wrath of the court. She wasn't unaffected by seeing me. I know she would be fine getting to know me.

If only she hadn't been wiped from my memory by the factory reset those jackals from the Barlowe family gave me. Lost in thoughts of revenge, I realize that hours have passed. The room is dark, and it is time to collect Olivia. Grabbing my bag from the bed, I take the stairs faster than I should, but the hall is empty, so no one will see. The car is out front, waiting. I get in and the driver sends the car gliding away from the curb. It seems an age before we stop before the doors of Roman's mansion. My steps are light as I walk to the door and knock. It opens almost immediately to allow me entrance. Just as the door closes behind me, a terrible howl sounds throughout the house.

The sound is filled with sorrow and pierces even my heart. I can't imagine who would be making that noise. I spot Olivia at the top of the stairs. She is crying even as she descends each step in a marked stride. Every line of her body says that she is forcing herself away from someone or something she desperately wants to stay with. Watching her, I realize it must have been her dog that made the noise. Why would she not have the dog with her? She draws near, and I tell her, "You can bring your dog, if you like. I don't mind, since we had dogs in the past. It isn't a problem."

A sob escapes her before she presses a fist to her lips.

Clearing her throat, she says, "No, I can't. Shut up, and let's get this over with."

Someone opens the door for her as she draws near it, and I follow her out. The small carry-on bag she has with her can't contain enough clothes to dress her through the year. "Do you not have any other bags?"

"They are sending anything they think I will need." She gets in the car without another word, and I can hear the howling again. I feel like a world-class asshole as I settle in the car. The driver smoothly guides us into traffic. I don't understand why she can't bring her dog. If she loves it that much, why not bring the damn thing with her? Maybe she thinks poorly of me for trying to make her leave the one that lay dying next to her? She is staring out the window, obviously determined not to speak to me. I heave a sigh of frustration. This is going nothing like I had hoped. I didn't expect gratitude, but she seems to be fully grieving. Reaching into my bag, I pull out one of her books and start reading. There is nothing I can do here that she will appreciate, so it will be better if I leave her be.

OLIVIA

We are in a jet flying to Italy when my phone chimes with a message. I've been staring out the window since I boarded. I suppose I should at least see who is messaging. Maybe it's Duncan with pictures of Nims? Pulling my phone out of the carry on, I see that it's Blair.

"Is your insurance paying for the rebuild?"

"The rebuild?"

"Your house. From the fire?"

"My house burned down? And it's being rebuilt? What?"

"Yeah, didn't you know? It burned down a few days ago, and the rebuild started today, as far as I can tell."

Those bastards. I bet they knew and kept it from me. Roman probably decided he would rebuild it and add in all the security he wanted before I return, so he doesn't have to ask me.

> "Thanks for letting me know. I have to go. I need to have a conversation about this."

> 😝 get'em.

Pulling up Duncan's number, I tap the message icon and type,

> "How's the rebuild going?"

I hit send, and immediately after the message says delivered, he calls me via video message. I tap answer, and he looks decidedly uncomfortable when his face pops up. "So, you heard about that?"

"I did hear about that. Why didn't you tell me?"

"You were already upset after the hearing. We found out right after we got back, and you ran up to Nims. We decided it was something that could wait. For now, here's Nims."

Her face fills the screen, and I want to hug her. I want to turn this stupid jet around and go back to my dog. My best friend. "Oh, hello, Nims! I miss you so much, sweet girl."

She whines and sniffs the phone, her nose filling the screen. I can hear Duncan telling her I am not in the phone, and the phone shows a video. She seems to understand, or I guess she does because she sits back, so she can see me again.

"Hi, sweetie. I miss you so much already. Is Duncan taking good care of you? You make sure to eat, and I'll do the same. I have to go. We are landing soon. I love you so much. Duncan, we'll talk again soon. Keep my sweet girl safe."

I hit the end-call button fast, as I don't want my Nims to

see me crying again. I hit the airplane mode button as the pilot's voice sounds over the speaker. Thank goodness for dark-colored handkerchiefs. And dark colored clothing.

As I clean my face, Callum says, "I really meant what I said. You could have your dog here with you. Get one of them to bring her."

"Shut up Callum. You don't know what you are talking about."

He sits down across from me. "You could tell me a more detailed answer instead of giving the same one again and again. I am your sire, so it is my job to protect you."

His attitude of 'I'll be your savior' pisses me off. I figured this shit out with Nims. Me and her, we didn't need some jackass to protect us. We need each other. Swallowing the lump in my throat, I tell him, "I don't need your protection. I had things handled where I was. I don't suppose you have noticed it, but it's been well over five years. She and I did just fine without you. What you have done is come in and wreck the fantastic life I had going. Don't expect that I will be trusting you, or seeing you as some sort of great help, because you showed up and forced me to come with you. That makes you a controlling asshole."

THE AIRPORT IS LOUD. EVERYONE SEEMS TO BE INCREDIBLY happy on vacation or visiting family. I'd like them all to fuck off and out of my way. Callum gets us through the madhouse in no time. Though, it seems excruciatingly long to me because I don't want to be here at all.

But here I am.

I feel like, one day, I am going to look back at this and laugh. Who else is suddenly thrown into the lap of luxury with all these old vampires, and right as life begins to fall apart? Me. Torn from my Nims into unequivocal luxury. I wanted to provide the grandest life for my dogs, and now that I have it, we don't have each other.

Callum opens a car door for me, and I realize we are transferring into a limo. It is nice and smells of old wood mixed with new car. An interesting choice for scents. Callum and two men slide in after me. The men sit across from me, with Callum crowding me in my seat. As we drive, he turns and says, "I need to prepare you for what is to come. I realize you don't want to talk to me, but when we arrive at the family estate, there is going to be a dinner."

Staring at him, I say, "I have had nice dinners before. I know how to behave."

He shakes his head. "This isn't a nice dinner. This is a vampire dinner. I am guessing the dinners with Roman's family are not organized in this way. Our family is different, since competition is heavily encouraged. Which has created a toxic atmosphere. You will be tested tonight, and verbal sparring is going to happen. You are going to need to put aside all of your feelings and focus on survival. They won't want you at the dinner, but they won't want anyone else to have you or your attention. How you perform tonight will decide your fate with this family."

"Why did you bring me here? Why not leave me where I had a good life? You swoop in and force me to leave my home to come deal with this? Are you fucking kidding me? Tell me more about these garbage people you thought I should definitely be connected to, or interested in trading my dogs for."

He gives me a brief biography about the various people I'll meet. His brothers sound like the guys everyone avoids in the bar. Perverts with little understanding of the concept of consent. His mother, though, sounds like she is not only misogynistic but controlling, vicious, and power hungry. If I understand correctly, his father hasn't spent much time at home since his darling wife tried to kill him on their honeymoon.

"Why doesn't your father divorce her? Or murder her?"

"The short answer is her family. The longer answer is our society doesn't see a spouse attempting to murder you as a reason to break the marriage contract. They, and many others of our kind, marry mostly as part of a familial alliance. If my father divorces her, it will break the contract. Unless he has a valid reason. Her trying to murder him and take over the family doesn't mean anything. She would have to try to hurt the family as a whole or people entrusted to the care of the family."

"Sounds like, if she attempts to hurt me, then you all can get rid of her. Is that why you brought me here? Is there hope that I could go home faster?"

Callum sighs and shakes his head. "I brought you here because you are a member of the family, even if you don't want to be."

"You didn't say I was wrong about what could happen if she tried to harm me. Ok, I can work with this. Are there rules about whether or not she is provoked?"

"Please do not provoke her. She is not to be trifled with, and she can have you killed. I would prefer it that I not lose status in the family because the only family I have ever created became lost and then, right after making it home, gets herself killed."

Chapter Four

OLIVIA

This dress feels wrong.

My luggage hasn't arrived yet, and I have nothing very nice to wear to dinner without it. Callum sent for this slinky, green dress. The thin straps feel like they are going to snap at any given moment. I have enough tape on my boobs to send a package around the world via an angry killer whale. I am going to hate myself when I remove it later. Thank fuck, they sent the wide tape. I guess they knew I would need something to strap things in and possibly save the gathering from seeing my chest fly out of the dress.

When Callum knocks on the door to the room he gave me, I am laying across the bed and wishing I was home. The door creaks open when I don't say a word, and he asks, "Why didn't you answer the door?"

"Because I was trying not to stretch this dress too much by inhaling that much air."

He chuckles. "It can't be that bad."

"Help me up, and you can see for yourself. I have to be careful about moving too much. It might feel like a massive amount of tape, but that doesn't mean it won't give way." He crosses the room and clasps hands with me before pulling me into a standing position. I can feel the tape complain as gravity pulls, but it holds, so I guess I have to go to the damn dinner. Callum's eyes are focused on my cleavage, and I mean, it does look really nice. "Were you aware that my eyes are actually up here?"

His eyes don't move as he says, "I am, but the view here is stunning." He drags his eyes up to my face. "You are going to stay right next to me. I didn't realize how this dress would fit you. Don't get me wrong, you are stunning. Not everyone here tonight is a good person. We'll go to my house tomorrow. For now, let's face the gauntlet."

The room falls silent as we enter, with everyone turning to look at us. Wouldn't be so unnerving if there was a single smile in the entire group. But no, they are hostile. Every one of them. A bell chimes, and they leave off staring to seat themselves. Callum guides me to the two seats that are still open and pulls the chair farthest from his mother. Before I can sit, she lifts a hand, saying, "No. I would have her next to me. It is my wish to get to know our new family member, now that she is finally arrived." She waits for me to be seated. "What took you so long to take your place in the family? Did you run away from your agreement? Perhaps, we should discuss a fitting punishment, rather than integration into the family."

"Mother, you know very well why she was not here. If anyone is to blame, it is the family that attacked me while I was on the diplomatic mission you assigned. We never found out why that happened. Have you, perhaps, heard anything recently? Mother?"

Her eyes flick away for only a second. "No, my son, we still have no further information. It seems it was nothing more than a tragic case of mistaken identity. Even so, your protégé should have searched for the family, at the very least. She seems lazy to have not even made the attempt."

Her eyes linger on me as she speaks. The malevolence rolling off her is nearly a physical thing, hitting me with each word. My own anger rises. Who does this woman think she is? Calling me lazy, just like my parents did so many times. Like the good people of the church. Every shred of anger and shame I felt all the times they said her words rises and spills out before I can stop it. "How would you suggest I seek out a family that I neither agreed to become part of nor knew existed? Waking to find my life changed in ways I did not understand, and you think I should have magically known who had done this, when I did not even know his first name? Your expectations are high, and your welcome is poor."

"How dare you speak so to me! I am the matriarch of this family. A family that you belong to, whether or not you like it. You will do your part as such. You can start by apologizing for your rudeness." She looks to Callum as I smirk. "You will take your brat to your home and train her to behave as befits a member of this family, or I will have her killed. Do you understand me?"

I open my mouth to speak, but Callum crushes my hand in his under the table. "I do understand, Mother. We will leave now, if you would like. Then we can start her training immediately."

"No. You will both finish the evening here. You may leave in the morning. Our family has a right to assess its newest member, even if she is poorly mannered."

Snickers echo down the table but are silenced by a glance from her. Her glare returns to me. "You will keep a civil tongue when you answer your betters, or I will have you flogged, and you can spend your first night home in pain as you heal slowly from the wounds. Do you understand?"

A part of me wants to tweak the old bitch's nose with a smart answer. Callum squeezes my hand under the table again, and I think better of it. "Yes. I understand."

The triumph on her face turns my stomach, and I snatch my hand from Callum's. People come in then, bearing dishes and serving food. Wine is poured. Over the rich smells of the meal, the scent of human blood in the wine sends hunger pangs through my body, even as the idea causes it to roil. She seems to sense my discomfort and raise her glass, "A toast to Olivia, newest member of the family. May she learn our ways and be always a benefit to the family."

Cries of 'hear, hear' come from all along the table. None sound friendly. A shiver runs down my spine as everyone drinks their wine. Lifting my glass and sipping, I struggle with the desire to drain the glass. One of the attendants steps up next to me and serves me with a portion of the food. I don't care about the food anymore. The man serving the food is human, and he smells like a fantastic meal. I catch myself inhaling his scent, and I realize she has set me up. She wants me to attack one of her attendants, so she can have me killed or punished harshly. Damn these people, and damn this place. The attendant moves away, and I release a breath I didn't realize I was holding.

This is going to be a long dinner.

I NEVER IMAGINED I COULD BE SO GRATEFUL TO LEAVE A dinner table, but here we are. Just as I am thinking escape is at hand, Callum steers me toward the same room the rest of them are entering. Son of a bitch. We have to mingle with these motherfuckers, too? At least there aren't any humans yet. The blood in the wine was enough to stir the craving, not to sate it. One of the men ahead says, "Ah, now we feast."

Fear spikes through me at what that might mean. As we enter the room, I see humans in various stages of dress, many seeming in bliss as members of the family drink from them. As I watch, one woman gives a little gasp as she realizes he isn't going to stop before she dies. Her eyes roll back, and she is gone, her body tossed off to the side. The vampire that did it turns and sees me watching. He smiles, his teeth still red with her blood.

Callum is talking with someone, so he hasn't noticed. I'm sure he is quite used to things like this happening here. Then, the man is in front of me, his hand gripping mine. "We haven't been introduced. My name is Tony. What is your name?"

My stomach is roiling. I can smell the blood on his breath. The blood of the woman he casually tossed aside like so much trash. "Olivia. Nice to meet you."

I try to tug my hand away, but his grip tightens as he guides my hand to his lips and presses a kiss to my knuckles. No reaction, no reaction. That is what he wants, is my reaction. Callum, look this way, asshole. Tony begins to release my hand but, then, grips it harder. "Oh, I've left a little of my dessert on you. Let me get that."

I watch in horror as his mouth opens, and his tongue emerges as he pulls my hand toward it. Suddenly, a hand covers mine and snatches it from Tony's grasp. Callum says, "What the fuck do you think you are doing? Keep your fucking hands to yourself, or you are going to lose them."

Tony snarls, "Who do you think you are? She belongs to the family, not you alone."

"Wrong. She is mine, and I am here for familial duty only, or I wouldn't subject her to the likes of you. Filthy pig."

Tony shoves me out of the way and sneers right up in Callum's face. "I think I'll make her mine before the week is out. You can't be with her every minute of the day."

His smug smile must have been too much for Callum as he grabs Tony by the throat, lifting him into the air before slamming him into the floor. The tiles crunch and pop as he lands, shards flying every which way. Callum's hand never left Tony's throat, despite piercing it and little tracks of blood are racing for the floor.

Tony is making gurgling sounds when the mother walks up. "Callum, you know how much I hate fighting in the house. Look at the damage you have done to the floors. Release him, now. He didn't mean it. He will stay away from your pet."

Callum removes his hand but leans down to Tony's face, saying, "Next time, I won't hear her until I rip your vocal cords out. And I'll make apologies to Diane for not hearing her, but you still won't have a throat, brother. Do not touch what is mine. Ever." When he stands and turns, all traces of civility have left him. "Diane, my Olivia and I will be excused for the evening. I am done here."

"You haven't been excused from our company yet, Callum."

He crosses the space so fast, I don't even see him move, but now he is in his mother's face, "Let me remind you, I answer only to my father. You are merely someone I tolerate for the sake of a marriage contract between the two of you. I live for the day that your greed causes you to break it. Good evening, Diane. We will leave in the morning to continue her training, as you suggested." He looks at me and holds out a hand. It is demanding, and I don't like it. But I am afraid of what he will do if I don't, so I reach out and take it, keeping it firmly in mind that he defied his mother and was working on killing someone for me. He yanks me to his side, releasing my hand as he does and sliding his arm around my waist. He gives me seconds to collect myself before he draws me along with him and out the door.

He is silent as we cross the open area to the stairs. Going up the steps, he allows me a little breathing room, though his arm does not leave my waist. We get to the top, and he starts talking. "I'm sorry I didn't notice Tony sooner. I would never have let him touch what is mine, and he knows it."

I raise a brow at his wording. "Well, I don't actually belong to you."

He has me against the wall, his body pressed against mine, his lips next to my ear. His voice is gravel as he says, "You belong to me. Whether you like it or not, every inch of you is mine." His head dips lower, and I hear him inhale before he lifts his head to press his lips against the spot just behind my earlobe. "I can hear your heart racing. I can smell the reaction to my body pressed against yours. Your body knows who its owner is, and you will, too. Next time you say I don't own you, I'll bend you over my knee and spank you."

I want to be mad at what he is saying, but when he said he would bend me over and spank me, my panties got wet, and my pussy clenched. Oh Jesus, what the hell is wrong with me? He asks if I understand him, and I want to say no, but I see Tony standing on the stairs, watching with a smirk. "Yes, I understand."

Callum pulls me away from the wall, and we continue toward our rooms. Then, he says loudly, "I let you watch, Tony. But I'll destroy you, if I find you have been anywhere near her."

Chapter Five

Callum

It has been two days since I took Olivia away from the family home. She has spent her time here, as far from me as she could. I've given her time to get accustomed to my presence and even let her take over a small study. She goes in there a little after dark every night. Tonight will be different, though. We will begin her training by midnight.

Leaving my suite of rooms, I amble toward the study she has taken over. I can hear the gentle clack of the keys on her computer as she taps them fast. She doesn't look up when I walk in, or even as I draw near. "Olivia."

She holds up a hand, palm out, in the universal hold sign. Then, she is back to typing.

Moving over to the bench she is sitting on, I seat myself and slide over toward her. The table is nice, but this doesn't feel like a very good setup for a person who wants to sit for hours while writing. I should find her a desk and a chair, so she can be more comfortable. Perhaps, I'll send for something tonight and surprise her with it when she comes in tomorrow.

Twenty minutes later she stops typing, taps the command-and-s-key combo, then closes her laptop. She flinches when she turns her head and realizes I am sitting next to her. "You didn't notice my presence? Should I be offended?"

She rolls her eyes at me. "Yes. Be offended and send me home from this place. We'll tell everyone that I am completely ruined as a protégé, and you relinquish all claims to me. Roman's family will be pitied for taking in damaged goods, and I will be happy to be left alone."

I can't help laughing at her speech. "Sorry, pet, you will still be mine, whether or not my family has any claim to you. May as well get right with the idea now."

"Whatever. Did you seek me out for a reason?"

"Yes. It is time we begin your training. There is a great deal you do not know about our society that you absolutely need to learn. We have these rules in place to keep our more base natures in check. Vampire wars risk revealing everyone to the world. Today, we visit my library, and you will have books to read. These books are only for our family. They have not only the rules of vampire society, but those of our family as well. We have only ever printed them ourselves. The family bought a small press many years ago, and we all learned how to expertly bind a book, so that we can each make our own copy to keep with us. Our laws, our rules. They have not changed in centuries of use because they work, and they keep us safe. You will learn them, and while you learn, you will also print your books and bind them."

Her eyes light up, but then her phone rings, and she answers it immediately. Duncan's face appears on the screen, "Hey love, I hope it isn't too early for you. Nims has been at me since the minute the sun went down."

"No, it's never too early for her. Put her on." Her face lights up tenfold when the dog appears on screen. She talks to it, as if it were human. Telling it everything that has happened, and how much she misses her Nims. The dog responds with barks and growls. I would swear she cut her eyes at me at one point. I notice that, for all her telling of events, she doesn't mention the part at the top of the stairs. She glosses over that, as if it never happened. Interesting. Eventually, the call is ended with tears on her part and promises of coming home soon.

She sits for a moment after the call ends, staring at the darkened screen. Touching her arm, I say, "Come, let's go get those books." She starts like she had forgotten my presence again and then nods. "So tell me, is this a new book, or one you were already working on?"

"A new book. I finished the last one a week ago."

"Hmm, after you," I tell her as we get to the door of the study. "May I ask what inspired you to write this one?"

She chuckles, saying, "A deep desire to watch Tony and Diane die in pain."

I laugh as we reach the library. Opening the doors, I motion for her to enter first. She manages a few steps in and stops, looking around in awe. "Holy shit. I've seen public libraries smaller than this, and bigger libraries with fewer books. This is amazing. How long have you been collecting these?"

"Since before I was turned a very long time ago. I'm sure you have a fair size library now. You seem to have done well for yourself."

The temperature between us drops several degrees. Her face is devoid of emotion as she says, "You know nothing about how I have done for myself. Don't make stupid assumptions."

Ouch. Things must not have been easy on her. "I would like to hear about it. If you are willing to talk about it."

She shakes her head no. "There is too much I can't tell you to be able to tell you any of the story. Do you mind if I look around the library?"

"No, treat it as your own." I fall into step with her as she heads for a set of shelves. "You can trust me, Olivia. I promise I will always take care of you. Your welfare is everything to me."

She snorts as she turns away from me to look at some books. I shadow her as she moves through the books. Her scent drives me to distraction the more I am around her. Perhaps it will calm down once she is fully mine? Until the incident with Tony, I didn't know how fully she has wrapped me around her finger. The light from a lamp frames her in a soft halo, and I feel stirrings of tenderness toward her. I haven't felt this way toward anyone. Ever. I watched people around me fall in love, suffer for it. Some of them even died. I was unmoved by it, or anything else, beyond a longing to feel passionately enough to go through that for them. Not once in all this time did I feel anything. It was my father's favorite trait of mine. Loyal, but unattached to anyone or anything.

All that changed the night I found her. Even then, the scent of her drew me in. She has three books in her arms now, and I think perhaps it may be time to steer her toward the book we came here to get. "Olivia, we should get back to the training."

"Oh, yes, we came here for that, didn't we? Sure." She puts the book she was looking at back in its space and faces me. Putting a hand on her elbow, I guide her to the stairs, and we navigate our way to the locked shelf, at the back of the upper floor. I pull the key out of my pocket and unlock it to reveal my copy of the book, resting on a velvet lined cushion. Reaching in, I pick it up and hand it to her. She puts it to her nose and inhales.

"I love the smell of old books."

"Well, you'll get to enjoy that one as you study it. And now, we'll get the machine started on printing your copy. Have you eaten tonight?"

"Oh, no. I'm not really hungry."

"When was the last time you ate?"

She shrugs and looks away. "I should put these in my room, if we are going to be working on book binding. Unless the printing is going to take very long?"

"It won't, and we will work on the binding. We are also going to eat before we start, as I haven't eaten today either, and I prefer to eat with company. I'll see you in the dining room." She looks less than enthused, so I tell her, "I will find you and bring you in there, if you aren't in the dining area in five minutes."

She sighs as she walks away, and I know she was planning to ditch the food. I hurry to the kitchen and ask my chef to create a light charcuterie type meal. Then, I head to the press, turning it on and setting it to do a run for this book. I make it to the dining area, and she is not there. I look at my watch, she walks in. I give in to the urge and say, "Good girl."

Her face scrunches into a scowl as she walks to the table. I pull out a chair for her, and she attempts to walk past me. Snaking one arm out, I catch her around the waist and pull her to me. Gods above and below, she feels so good.

"Let go of me!"

"Sure." Lifting her off her feet, I turn and place her in the chair. "You were passing by your seat. I was only trying to help."

I think the smile on my face may have given me away, but she stays in the seat, even as she glares at me. "You are awfully pushy for someone who wants my cooperation."

"Aw, darling. I don't want your cooperation. I demand it." Leaning back in to inhale her amazing scent, I say, "And you liked it. You can lie and say you didn't, but we both know the truth. Your scent doesn't lie."

Stepping back and straightening, I move to my seat across from her. It's interesting how, even though we vampires don't have the ability to blush, the chemical release of adrenaline still happens, and we can smell it. I wonder if that is another thing she didn't know. It must be. How did she survive through this last decade? One of the kitchen staff brings our food out, setting dinnerware before us and the serving dish between us.

We are both silent as we select the bits we want to eat. She takes a bite of the food after I stare pointedly at her for a minute. I can almost hear her grumbling in her head about me. "Tell me about what happened when I didn't show up. You know why I couldn't be there. What happened? How did you get by? How did you figure things out?"

She looks up from her plate. I would swear I see a spark of fear in her eyes before she closes everything away. "I just did. How isn't your concern, so worry about yourself. Are you sure you want me to create a book? The chance of me staying part of this family is slim. They all want me gone. Why don't we just admit this will not work and send me home?"

Her words hit me like a hammer. What nerve is this hitting? "You are staying here. Yes, I want you to create a book. Whatever the result, I wanted the opportunity to spend this time training you. I understand why you wouldn't want to be part of the Mezzasalma family. We were not always this way. My father made what he felt was an advantageous marriage alliance that turned out to be other than he planned. The book will be yours, and when the year is done, I will take you back to Inverness." She is watching me with narrowed eyes. No trust lingers in her. Good. "I will stay in Inverness as long as you do. You can get rid of the rest of the Mezzasalma, but you will never be done with me."

Her mouth falls open. It is adorable. "What if I want you to go away? What if I need you to go away?"

Didn't expect that. Damn. I wonder. "Why would you need me to go away?"

"Don't you worry about that. Being as you are essentially holding me hostage, you don't get to know things about my life. You don't get to know my secrets. This is the cost of forcing me to be here with you. You are choosing this, and I will not forget that."

Fuck.

Chapter Six

BLAIR

The note appeared on the counter in my kitchen moments ago. I know the witches sent it. I can smell their magic. One more sip of my coffee to fortify me, and I reach over to pick it up. The paper practically jumps into my hands with a weird little sigh. It unfolds in my hand, a summons from the witches. I say, "I will be there soon."

The paper folds itself again and disappears. Their magic is fascinating and seems useful in a great many ways. I don't know if I would care to have the responsibility of it, though. A sip of my coffee. Oh, yuck. It's gone cold. How long was I lost in thought about witches' powers? Setting the cup down, I head for the door. It's never a good idea to keep witches waiting. They have funny ideas about what is offensive and ways to curtail offensive behavior.

It takes minutes to walk to the witch's store in the morning. A fair amount of the magical area isn't interested in mornings, and the ones that are don't often want to come out into the market area. The witch's store is open, doors propped to let in the light, and any customers who might be about. The witch at the counter gestures to the door to the back room when I walk in. It opens, and I head for that. Like many of those non-morning witches, she appears to be unhappy about the early shift. Sometimes, the best thing a person can do is shut up, and do what they are told. I see an open door with light spilling out. If I had to guess, I would say that is probably Ailsa's office. She is sitting at her desk, waiting when I walk in. Her brow furrows as she stares down at a collection of rocks and things laid on her desk, like they were tossed there.

"You sent for me?"

She looks up as if surprised to find me here. "Yes, come in. Shut the door."

I do as she says and sit in front of her desk. She swipes the pieces into a cloth bag and sets them to the side before she focuses on me. "I think things are not going so well for Olivia. Being apart from her family and Nims, mostly Nims, is doing things to her that could change things for the worst."

"I agree. She needs Nims with her, but I don't know what we can do about it. The vampire court has ordered her to live with him."

"I am aware. There are things I can do about that, but I would prefer not to start a war."

"Are you worried that vampires would win?"

She laughs, her head thrown back, and for a moment I can see how beautiful she is, when she isn't trying to be so severe and serious. I wonder why she makes herself seem so? Her laughter dies off, and she says, "No. Not only do we provide the majority of their food source, but also we provide places for them to hide and be themselves. All that doesn't touch on the fact that we can eliminate them without leaving our homes."

"Sure is a good thing you all are fond of dogs." She looks

confused, and I tell her, "Shifters are majority wolves, which are just bigger, wilder dogs. I figure that, and our tendency to have a pack mentality towards being part of the magical community in general, gives us a better chance of survival. Maybe you won't delete us because we are cute."

She laughs again, holding herself as she falls back in her chair. When she sits up again and wipes tears from her eyes, she says, "I haven't laughed so hard in a very long time. Thank you." The door opens behind me, and her eyes flick up before coming back to me, her face a mask of serious again. "And that is the end of this meeting. The world calls, and I must answer. We may send you to her, if things continue as they are. Prepare for it. Tend to your affairs. We would send you in a protective bubble. The vampires there will not be able to touch you." The shock may have shown on my face because she continues on. "We cannot lose her, and there is a tipping point. She isn't there, yet."

"I'll be ready this afternoon. I wouldn't mind being sent before I am needed. She, she means a lot to me, and I don't want to lose her either."

"We will let you know when it is time."

/ Chapter Seven

Olivia

"Olivia. Wake up Olivia, we've been missing a part of your training. Olivia." His words call me out of a dream, where I am with my Nims in our house, into the lush confines of his castle.

Without opening my eyes, I ask, "Why are you here? I was happy there."

"I'm here because we have missed a part of your training. The reason the sun has so much effect upon you is that you missed the time you should have spent drinking my blood."

My eyes fly open at this. He is only an inch from my face. "What do you mean, saying I should have been drinking your blood?"

"I mean, in the normal course of things, you would have been drinking my blood for the first few weeks. To mature you as a vampire. By the end of that time, which new vampires are meant to serve, you wouldn't have been affected by the sunlight so much."

Nims. "And could any vampire fill that role? If say the one that made them wasn't around to do it?"

His eyes narrow as he looks at me. "Yes, they could. But it will work faster, if it is the one that turned them. Do you wish to feed lying down or sitting up?"

"What is the difference?"

"My position. If you wish to feed lying down, then I will need to be on top of you, letting you feed from my neck. If you sit up, I can sit behind you, and let you feed from my arm."

A picture of him on top of me flashes through my mind, and I am instantly aroused. "I'll sit up."

"What a shame. Very well."

I move to adjust up, and I remember how I went to sleep. Naked. Grabbing for the sheet, I hold it to my chest, tucking it around behind me once I am upright. His smirk tells me he was fully aware I was not dressed. "Slide forward, so I can sit behind you."

Doing as he says, I sit very straight while he seats himself behind me. I can feel the coolness of his body, then an arm snakes around my belly, and he pulls me back to sit flush against him. My breath catches in my throat. I feel every inch of him pressed against my back. Including the part that is rapidly growing rock hard. Why, oh why, does the one guy I need to get away from for the safety of Nims have to be one that sends fire straight to my core? He brings his arms up in front of me and unbuttons his sleeve. Watching him roll it up is almost mesmerizing. Those arms... focus, Olivia. Focus.

He has finished rolling up his sleeve and is holding his left arm in front of me. His mouth is right next to my ear as he says, "Go ahead, take a drink. I promise I won't bite, unless you ask me to." Great, now I have thoughts of him biting me running through my head. I squirm a little, and he chokes. "I would appreciate it if you did not squirm against my erection, unless, of course, you would like to help me with it."

"Sorry. And no, I am not helping with it." No matter how much I want to. Resisting the urge to squirm, I put my hands on his arm and pull it to my mouth. Closing my eyes, I sink my teeth into his flesh. He tastes of dark delights and heat. His blood warms me and seems to quench a thirst I didn't realize I had. He moans behind me, sounding tortured. I release his arm, and he sighs. "Are you okay? Did I hurt you?"

He leans back against the headboard. "Oh, you hurt me in the most delicious way. I wouldn't mind if you did it again."

"Oh. I see." Leaning forward, I gather myself to stand, so he can get up, but his arms wrap around me and pull me back to lie against him. His erection digs into my back.

"If you stand up, I am going to see much more of your backside than you intended. And as the curve of your back was already tormenting my eyes with the desire to see more, I think it best if you stay seated, and I force myself to move out of this spot. Though, I would happily stay here, holding you and suffering the pain of having this gorgeous body of yours so close, though I can do nothing more than hold it." He has one hand on my chest above my breasts and the other on my belly. Everything in me aches for him to move those hands down. He sighs, "It helps not at all how turned on you are. Send me away, if you are going to. I don't know how much longer I can take this."

Swallowing hard to move the lump in my throat, I say, "Um, yes. Please, leave."

His hands leave my body immediately. After I sit up, he lifts himself off the bed. Turning back to me, he leans in. I lean back to keep him from being so close, and he follows till my head touches the pillows. He stops a breath away. "Sleep well. I'll feed you again tomorrow. Maybe if you are a good girl, I'll wait till you are in bed again and leave you ready to pleasure yourself." He leans down a little further, moving his face to be near my neck as he inhales. Then, he whispers, "Unless you change your mind and let me help you with… your desires."

Need spikes through me, and I bring my hands up, shoving him away. "You should go to your room. I'll see you tonight."

He grins at me. "As you wish. Sleep well."

He strolls out, closing the door gently behind him. I wait long enough for him to be away from the door before I spread my legs, and allow my fingers to take care of the fire he started.

Chapter Eight

Callum

I haven't seen her yet tonight. I wonder where she is hiding? Not in the library. The corridor to her room smells of her. As I draw near, I can hear her voice. Her door is open, and she is talking to someone, telling them how much she loves them. How she misses them. Rage floods my body. What is this? Am I jealous? Is that what this is? Every word she says to them is filled with love. I want that from her. I need it. And here she is, just giving it to some jerk that couldn't even keep her from me. A dog barks and makes noises, deflating all my jealous rage as I realize she is having her evening chat with her Nims.

I lean against the wall near her door, waiting. Rubbing my tongue on the sharp edge of my tooth is soothing in a lot of ways. That little sharp edge of pain, the taste of blood, centers me. Centers any emotion I am feeling. Her nails down my back as she comes on my cock might have the same effect.

The pictures in my head take off. Olivia bent over the railing of the stairs. Spread out on my bed as bury my face between her thighs. Against the wall behind me. Riding me with wild abandon.

"Callum. Callum!" Coming back from pretty fantasies, I turn to see Olivia standing just outside her door, hands on those glorious hips, and a glare pointed at me as she says, "What are you doing hovering in the hall outside my bedroom? With a hard-on? What the hell?"

Damn, did not intend for that to happen. "Apologies. I was seeking you for the evening feeding. When I heard you on the phone, I decided not to disturb you, and I tuned out the conversation. But then my mind wandered into thoughts of you. The results of that are this." I gesture toward my raging hard on.

She smiles and looks away. She is going to forgive me. If only she would also help me out with the current issue of my cock throbbing with need for her. Ugh. Awful, unsexy thoughts. What is that game the Americans are so fond of? Football! Yes. Tons of angry Americans stuffed into stadiums to watch the game. Very reminiscent of the gladiator games with less immediate death. "Come, let's go for a walk. You can feed when we get back."

As we walk the estate, she calms and eventually asks, "How did you get from seeking me for a feeding to the other?"

"When I walked up, I heard you talking so sweetly, and I initially thought you were talking to a man. I felt an intense jealousy for a brief moment, until I realized you were talking to the dog." She has turned her face away and I feel certain she is amused. "At that point, I was trying to relax, and my mind was already on you. Needless to say, it wandered into dangerous territory."

"I'm dangerous territory now?" She gives a little laugh, "If I were dangerous I wouldn't have the problems I have."

We are nearly to the castle when she utters those words, and I grab her arm, stopping her with me and stepping in front of her. Using one finger, I tip her chin up to look at me. Her breathing is suddenly rapid, and her arousal fills the air. Focus. "I know the court thing didn't inspire any trust in me, but I promise you, I want only the best for you. Your safety is my problem. Your problems are my problems. Let me help you."

She shakes her head. "Really? Because my top of the pile problem is being here. I need to go home. Are you going to let me? Let me be free to live my life? Release me from this ridiculous ruling that I have to be here? Will you let me go, Callum?"

Her words pierce my heart like tiny daggers. "I can't let you go. But, I can take you home soon. Would that help? Would it help if we stay in your home?"

She looks like she might cry as she says, "Really? You'll take me home? You aren't toying with me?"

"No, I am not toying with you. We do have to finish some things before we leave. We are both required to attend the ball here. There is no getting around that. But, after that, I will take you home, so you can be with your Nims, even though you refuse to tell me why you can't just bring her with you."

She throws her arms around me and hugs me. "Thank you! Thank you! That's all I need, to be home with my Nims." She loosens her grip to lean back, "When is the ball here?"

"A week. When we pack to go to the family house, you will pack everything of yours and we will send what you don't need to your home. I will buy what I need when we arrive."

She hugs me again and, as my arms are wrapped around her, I think I would burn this castle to the ground if she asked it of me. She says, "Thank you. I really can't explain how much this means to me. I'm going to tell Nims, Duncan, and Blair later. They are all going to be so excited."

"It gives me joy to please you. Come, let's get you fed. We can do that in the library, and then you can search out the books about us."

"You want me to find books? Wonderful. Let's go." She releases me, and I feel a pang as she pulls away. Then, she turns, reaches back, and grabs my hand. "Come on."

I let her tug me along, pleased that she wants to hold my hand. As we enter the house, my mother's butler is there, waiting. I watch his eyes focus on our joined hands and his lip curls. He zips over and snatches her away from me, saying, "How dare you."

And then, I send him flying across the room. A sickening crack resounds between the walls as he hits one of them head first. All I care about is her, standing there, frozen.

"Are you ok?" A few steps brings me to her, and I check her arm.

"Is he human?"

"Who?"

"Oh, I don't know. Maybe the man you threw across the room?"

"No. He'll get up shortly, and he'll know from now on that putting his hands on you has consequences."

"Why would you do that?"

"Because he touched you. No one touches you without your consent. And I really liked you holding my hand and tugging me along behind you."

"I don't know that you really needed to throw him against the wall like that."

"It's fine." I hear him groan and rustle around as he

maneuvers himself into a standing position. "See, he's getting up. And he won't forget that touching you is forbidden."

"Indeed," Graham says as he brings himself fully erect. "Protocol."

"I have other walls, Graham. I am happy to introduce you to each of them. She is mine, and I am completely hers." Her jaw drops as I say that. "You should apologize to her, Graham. She is the lady of this house any time she resides here."

He is silent, so I turn my head to look at him. He casts his eyes to the floor. "Apologies, ma'am. I shouldn't have touched you without permission. It won't happen again."

"Very good. Why are you here?"

"Your mother requests your presence at the house, at least two days before the ball."

"Did she give a reason?"

"She requires your help with the preparations."

"We will arrive after dark, two days before the ball, and no sooner. See yourself out." I watch him leave the room, and I turn back to Olivia, "Are you ok? He didn't frighten you too bad? Come," I slip my arm around her shoulders, "let's go to the library. A feeding will settle you, and then, you can search the books."

She looks up at me like I am making no sense, but she allows me to guide her. Once there, she stops and says, "How are we going to do this?"

For my answer, I scoop her up and walk over to the closest chair. As I seat myself, I settle her on my lap. "We can do this one of two ways. You can feed from my arm or my neck. What do you prefer?"

"Well, what do you prefer? I am biting you. At the very least, it should be in the place you prefer."

"Neck. Definitely the neck." She nods and stands.

Turning to face me, she puts a knee to either side of me and lowers herself to sit on my thighs. It is bliss and torture, and I never want it to stop.

"Which side?"

"This one," I say as I tip my head to the left, exposing the right side of my neck. My fingers fly to my shirt, unbuttoning the first four buttons and pushing the right side away. She nods and leans in. I can feel her breath on my neck, the slight sting as she sinks her teeth in. She drinks so delicately, sipping rather than mauling. Her tongue moves against my neck, the sensation derails my efforts to keep my dick out of this. It engorges, pressing against my pants and the juncture of her thighs. Gods, the torment. Holding still is painful as my cock throbs and begs to be pressed harder against her. Then, she moans, and her hips rock against me. Shit, the hormones of my arousal must be hitting her. Tapping her shoulder once signals her to release. She sits back, her pupils dilated, a hint of red on her lips, and the flush of feeding in her cheeks. Her hands massage my shoulders, and her hips rock a little. The friction is delicious, and I want to pursue this to fulfillment, but I can't. "Good gods. Olivia, you have to stop." Her back arches, breasts pushing toward my face. My mouth opens as I lean in. No! "Olivia, you're killing me."

She undulates, rubbing against my cock again. My eyes roll back in my head as she presses harder, leaning in to whisper, "I know. Let's fix the problem. I've always wanted to have sex in a library."

"Oh, hold on to that thought for another day. I was aroused while you were feeding, and the hormones are affecting you."

Her lips are a hair from my ear, her hands unbuttoning my shirt as she says, "I know. It was amazing to feel how turned on you were by me. I've never known exactly how turned on a person is by me, and I found it intoxicating. Please, let's do this now. Please. I want you. I promise I know exactly what I am doing."

How can I say no to such sweet begging? Grabbing her hands, I pull them behind her back, where I use one hand to hold both her wrists behind her. Her back arches, her breasts pressing against my face. My free hand goes to the bottom of her shirt, dragging it up over her breasts. They are nearly spilling out of their lacy cups. Slipping one finger in to the side and sliding it along the top edge of the cup while pulling out and down has her sucking air through her teeth as her breast is released from its confines. Licking my lips, I take that dusky nipple in my mouth, sucking hard. She cries out, pressing her chest further into my face. My free hand trails down her back, stopping to cup that luscious ass of hers.

She tries to move one of her arms, and I give her nipple a little nip. Her moan is music to my ears. I let that nipple go and bury my face between her breasts, inhaling her scent.

Olivia

"Callum, please." He ignores my plea and moves to the other breast. His mouth feels hot as it closes around my lace covered nipple. His tongue is dancing across it, over and over. The throbbing in my pussy is growing. I can't help but to grind against his cock as much as possible with my arms held behind me. The way he has them imprisoned in one hand, I had never realized how hot that would make me. His arm goes around my waist, and he stands, holding me tightly against himself. I feel so exposed as he gently lifts my shirt over my head and slides it down my arms. Just when I think he is going to remove it entirely, he uses it to tie my wrists together. I've never let anyone do this before, but it feels so fucking right with him. His hands freed, he uses one to pull the other cup of my bra under my breast. He pinches the nipple, and I clench my thighs for some relief from the throbbing between them.

His mouth covers that nipple, his hair tickling my chest. I can feel his hands working the fastening of my pants. Then, he releases my nipple with a pop as he drops to his knees before me. He pulls my pants off with an agonizing slowness. Pressing a kiss to my mound, he brings his hands back up and pulls the panties down. Every inch of my body is on fire for this man. Why do I want him so much? Then, his mouth is on my lips, tongue sliding between them to tickle at my clit. My ankles are trapped in my pants, and I can't spread my legs to give him better access. I can't stop the moans of pleasure as his tongue manages to work magic. As the pressure is at a peak, just before I explode, he stops. I could cry with the agony of it. When he lifts my leg, releasing me from the trap of my pants, my excitement builds. He grips my hips and says, "Sit on the arm of the chair."

In a move completely out of character for me, I do exactly what he says. He gently places one of my feet in the chair's seat before he buries his face between my thighs. Seconds later, I am soaring over the cliff's edge, my orgasm so intense I nearly fall off the chair's arm.

He catches me, holding me in place as his mouth continues to feast upon me. The sensations just keep building till I am screaming with it. "Oh god, Callum! Callum, I can't take any more! Callum!"

His tongue stops for a moment and he says, "You'll take it till I have had my fill of this delicious pussy."

My mind is racing as the waves hit me again. I cry out, "What about you? Let me please you."

He chuckles, the vibration of it sending me over again. Afterward, he stands. "Very well, I can deny you nothing. Ask, and it is yours. Will you please me with that pretty mouth of yours? Or should I bend you over the back of this chair and fuck you senseless?"

He drops his shirt and is working on his pants as he speaks. They drop to the floor, and his cock is standing out, big and proud. Thankfully, it doesn't look like it would murder me. I think my pussy needs a minute to collect itself, so I tell him, "Mouth."

It's a little strange to have my hands tied as he asks me where I want it, but here we are. I can't say I'm sad about it or any kind of upset. He steps closer and puts his own hands behind his back, saying, "You'll direct this. I won't move unless you tell me to."

I don't understand it, but him saying that releases some fiend in me, and I just want to make him beg. I pull my hands out of the shirt as I lean forward, mouth open, to swirl my tongue around the head. Dear god, does all vampire cock taste this good? It's sweet, with just a hint of a citrus scent. His moans are like a drug for me. I want more. He is true to his word, hands locked behind his back. I can see the muscles straining. I step up my ministrations, and he cries out, "Olivia, it's, I can't, I'm going to come."

That same fiend in me wants to make him come now, and I pick up the pace. He shouts as he explodes in my mouth. Holy hell, it's nothing like human come. This tastes faintly of sugar and oranges. It's not completely that, but it's enough that I surely don't mind. When I have gotten every last drop, I lean back, fairly satisfied with my evil deeds.

He looks down at my half grin and smiles, "You think we've finished? Oh, Precious, we've just begun."

He looks around the library and nods. Then, he reaches

out and grabs my hands, tugging me up into a standing position, he says, "Come over here."

He leads me to a desk covered in various writing tools and, with a sweep of his arm, a space is cleared. He guides me to the end of the desk and tells me, "Put a knee up here. Don't worry, I'll keep you from falling."

Even before he reassures me, I am doing what he said. What is wrong with me? Why am I so willing to do anything he says when it's about sex? Oh god, oh no. It can't be.

He pushes into me in one smooth thrust, his cock filling me. Hitting that spot inside. "Oh, fuck me, that's the spot."

He chuckles and starts fucking me with a nice rhythm. My hands hit the desk to hold me up, and I am just melting into the tabletop. His hands are grasping my hips as he fucks me harder. It's so good, and suddenly I am coming again, my legs shaking like crazy. He speeds up and slams into me one last time, holding himself so very still as he comes with me. Fuck me, I am in so much trouble. How is it even possible I care for this guy?

Duncan and Blair are waiting at home. I need to go think. Something must be wrong with me. A knock sounds at the door, and he has a blanket wrapped around me before I can do more than gasp.

Callum

She ran away as soon as my employee finished telling us that dinner was ready. Up to her room, where she locked herself in, and she only opened the door to allow them to give her the dinner I sent up. I can hear her crying. It's breaking my heart, and I don't know what to do. How do I fix this? I knew we shouldn't have sex yet. Knew she wasn't ready. I just couldn't resist her. Can't deny her anything. That's why we are leaving as soon as the ball is over. Not because it won't complicate the fuck out of things.

The family is going to be pissed about my flouting of traditions. Father is going to be irate. He specifically told me to keep her here. I still don't understand why he cares so much about where she stays. I wonder what exactly is Mother Dearest up to?

Pulling out my phone, I tap the screen to bring up her name and hit call. She shrills in her smooth, not-so whisper, "Callum, how nice to hear from you."

"No, it isn't. What are you up to? I know you are plotting something. What the fuck is it?"

"I am plotting a great, many things as the current de facto head of the family. Since your father refuses to come home."

"Indeed. It's like he wants to live. What are you scheming regarding Olivia? Why are you so insistent that we attend the ball? That I help you with the setup?"

She laughs. "Careful, Callum, you are revealing too much. I might think you care about her. We want you and her close because she was never properly introduced to or made part of the family. I want to make her feel welcome."

"I see. So, Father is on the judging panel right now. That explains a lot. What is it you want with her?"

"Want? Whatever could we want from a woman that writes horror and spends the rest of her time rounding up stray dogs? If anything, we expect to get her trained up, so that she doesn't shame the family, since it is known she is one of us. Callum, I am fully aware of the adoption petition put forth by the Slora family. She must be tested, so we know if she is worth staking a claim over. It would shame the family for us to release the claim on her, only to find out she could be useful."

"She isn't useful. She's nothing. Just a silly girl, in over her head. Her time here has demonstrated how unfit she is to be a part of the family. She wasn't even capable of handling one night with us. I will request she is released to the Slora family at the next hearing."

"Ah, she is that important to you? Excellent. Don't forget that you are expected to come and help with the preparations. Make sure you bring your little toy. See you both soon." Her laughter rings in my ears for long moments after she ends the call.

Shit.

Chapter Nine

His door is open as I approach. I figure I owe him an apology for refusing to talk to him after our little feed fest. I stop short of knocking when I hear him speaking. "She isn't useful. She's nothing. Just a silly girl, in over her head. Her time here has demonstrated how unfit she is to be a part of the family. She wasn't even capable of handling one night with us. I will request she is released to the Slora family at the next hearing."

His words are like daggers in my heart. I run away from his door as quietly as I can. I don't need him knowing that I know exactly how he feels about me. I don't stop running til I am safe in my bedroom. Leaning against the closed door, I just shake my head. God, I'm so stupid. So stupid.

Locking the door, I go to the window. I didn't even realize it was raining. I just want to be home and walk my dog in the rain. Did he even mean it when he said he would take me home after the ball? He has to. He just has to. The phone calls with Nims aren't enough. I feel like I'm slowly suffocating here. Even before this, I could feel myself stretching, like an elastic pulled too tight.

I have to believe he will take me home. He has to, because I don't know if I will survive here.

CALLUM

I haven't seen her since yesterday. When I fed her and things got out of hand. It is time again. She'll have no choice but to see me. Stopping outside her bedroom door, I knock. Silence answers me, and I knock again. Still nothing and my patience is wearing thin. Perhaps a spanking is exactly what she needs. I try the knob, and it isn't locked. I know before I open it that she isn't in there. Her room is neat, but I can still smell traces of her.

Closing the door, I start for the gardens. It is still raining, but she might have gone out there, anyway. It isn't as if we will melt for being in the rain. I don't see or smell her anywhere in the house. The rain interferes with my sense of smell, filling the air with other scents and dampening everything else. Long minutes later, I find her sitting next to a small pond, watching the koi swim.

She doesn't look up at my approach. I sit down next to her, and she looks over, crinkling her brow and frowning. "What do you want?"

"It is time for your feeding. Do you want to do it here or in the house?"

"Here is fine."

"Arm or neck?"

"Arm."

Unbuttoning the cuff and rolling up my sleeve, I extend

my arm toward her. She grasps it just below the elbow and leans forward. I watch her lips draw near to my arm, my cock twitches in anticipation. She bites me viciously, and I suck air through gritted teeth. "You are playing a dangerous game."

She releases my arm and wipes away traces of blood from her lips. "When will this stop? When will this feeding be done?"

"It will be done when you can tolerate the sun. Ordinarily, the process would have taken a few years, but as you have been a vampire for a decade, it probably won't. We can't be sure until we check, as this is not how it usually works. You should have been with me, and I am so sorry I was not there for you."

She sighs and says, "The past doesn't matter. I appreciate your apology. We leave for the family house tomorrow night, right?"

"Yes. We will be there for two nights and then leave for Scotland. Are you ready to study?"

"Let's get this over with."

After separating to dry and change clothing, we meet in the library again. She grabs the book she was studying when we met last and sits, holding the book at just the right angle to avoid eye contact with me. How do I fix this? We were moving forward until we had sex here. Fuck. Maybe we should have our lessons in a different room from now on. Except, it won't matter. We are leaving, and she won't see this room again anytime soon. Perhaps she will feel more at ease when she is reunited with her dog.

There is something strange about it. It has something to do with what she has been keeping from me. What could it be? The dog looks fairly young. She can't have had it long enough to be so attached to it, unless she falls hard for dogs? She had that one the night when I found her. Perhaps she gets a similar dog each time and begrudges any time that she can't spend with them because of how short their lives are?

She shifts in her seat, and I realize that sunrise is upon us. She is nearly finished with the book she started reading. It takes everything in me not to stare, as she is so lovely, her face set as she focuses on the last page of the book. I clear my throat as she gets close. She frowns while she ignores me to read the last line, then allows her attention to land on me.

"The sun has risen. Do you want to check?"

Her eyes widen and she nods. Rising, I walk over to the window and slide the curtain back. She stands and stretches before walking across the room, stopping just outside of the sunlight. Stepping through the front row of beams, I come to stand behind her, ready to snatch her away from the light. She extends her hand slowly, creeping toward the rays of the sun. My hands move toward her as she draws near to a possible injury. Her fingers enter the sun, and nothing happens. She stares at them for long moments in silence before she bursts into tears.

I pull her into my arms. "Why are you crying? This is a good thing."

She pushes out of my arms. "You wouldn't understand, and you can't know about it. You cannot be trusted with this."

Grasping her arms, I snatch her to staring me in the face. "What secrets are you keeping from me? Share them. I promise I will keep them, and you, safe."

She glares up at me, "No. Mind your fucking business."

Something in me snaps, and I lift her, keeping her arms pinned against her. I lean in, soaking up the scent of her.

"Every part of you is my business." She shudders as a tear tracks its way down her face. I kiss the drop from her jaw. Sighing, I tell her, "I haven't time to pry your secrets from you today. For now, you are still young enough that you need sleep. Go sleep and be ready to leave tonight by eight tonight. We don't need to concern ourselves with making sure the sun is gone so we can arrive there as darkness falls. While we are there, there are rules for your safety. I know I've told you this already, but your safety is everything. No wandering off by yourself, no matter how mad at me." I lean in to inhale her scent. "We present a united front. In everything. I will only usurp your decision making for reasons of safety. I know things about all of these people that you do not, and I do not, have enough time to tell you all of it as I have learned it over hundreds of years. Most importantly, do not eat anything that you do not see my mother eating. Her specifically, she is willing to sacrifice anyone, and everyone for her goals." She nods and I release her. "Go, sleep. I'll see you tonight."

She nearly runs from me, away from the desire I know she feels. I can smell her arousal for all that she is running from it. If only I knew what she is hiding from.

Chapter Ten

Everything is packed. Boxes stand ready next to the door, waiting to be shipped home. Home. I can't wait to see my Nims, to hug her fuzzy neck. Closing the one suitcase I am taking with me, I haul it off the bed and head for the car downstairs.

Callum waits near the front door. I know it when he feels my presence because his head turns, and his eyes are on me. He is next to me before I finish blinking and offering, "Let me take that for you. Are you ready? Have you got your dress packed?"

I release my suitcase because I know trying to keep it is futile. "Yes, my dress is packed, and I am ready. Did you have the same shop send this one?"

He nods as he puts an arm around me, resting his hand on my hip. "I did. With better directions, and an insistence that they fit it to your measurements."

My lips lift in a half smile. "So, I won't need to tape my chest to the heavens and pray it holds?"

He chuckles. "That is the idea. Though, I would love to see you in that dress without the tape sometime."

"Keep dreaming. That is not happening again."

"Happens every time I dream, and you think about it every time I am close to you."

I snatch my elbow out of his grasp. "Keep your hands, and your damn nose, to yourself."

He laughs as he opens the door and holds it for me. I sail on through and climb into the waiting car. He hands off my suitcase to the man holding the door and follows me in, sliding over to sit next to me. I ask, "Must you sit so close? I would prefer some space."

"Yes, and you need to pretend you like it. Because this is what we are going to do the entire time we are at the family house. We are going to be really cozy. You will have time alone in the evening, as your room will be separate from mine, aside from the open door between us. And that will stay open. It is for your safety. I will respect your privacy and not interact with you while we are in our rooms, unless you are in trouble or initiate otherwise. Think you can handle that?"

"I guess. When do we leave?"

"We travel to Scotland the morning after the ball. You will be able to sleep on the plane. I took the risk that you would be willing to stay up late, in order to leave sooner. Should I change the flight time?"

"No! That is good. We can't leave the ball early? Can we?"

"Sadly no. Mother means for me to be the host. We won't be able to leave till morning at the earliest."

The drive to the family estate is quick, and we arrive before I can respond to when we can leave. As soon as we get inside, the entire family is waiting. It's creepy. They whisk us off to dinner. This time, we are at least prepared for his mother's insistence that I sit next to her. After we are seated, she looks me up and down. Her face selects her usual mask of disapproval, and she asks, "Have you learned to keep a civil tongue in your head?"

Callum's hand grips mine as I reply, "Yes. Callum's teaching has been beneficial in many ways."

The grip of his hand eases, and his thumb strokes the back of my hand. It feels so nice, and I hate it. His mother tells me I should find a woman to ask about doing my hair, so that I don't embarrass the family. Tugging my hand out of his grip, I tell her, "I will try to find someone. It is short notice, and I am sure you and others in the family have already scheduled the best for themselves."

Her eyes narrow, and she says, "Some of us have enough experience to not need a hairdresser. While you are at it, find someone to do your makeup. It isn't seemly for a vampire to look so pink all over."

Callum cuts off any response I would have made, saying, "That's odd, Mother, you have Francois work miracles with creating a pink and healthy complexion every year. It's almost like you dislike the idea of competition."

Diane glares at him. "Insolent boy! Do not interfere in my games again."

Callum puts an arm around my shoulders and pulls me, and my chair, closer to him. The closeness of his body ignites mine on fire. He is responding to her, but I am having trouble focusing on his words. Inhaling to clear my head is a mistake, since all I can smell is him. He gives my shoulder a squeeze, and that helps to bring me to reality, and the conversations around me dial back into focus.

Diane's glare glides over to me. "Have you drugged her, Callum? Is that why she cannot control her response to you and emits that stench at my table?"

Callum smirks as he gestures down the table. "You may not appreciate the scent of her lust, but it would appear that the rest of the family does."

Horrified, I look down the table to see they are all staring at me. Oh God, this is awful. They all know what I was thinking about, that I can't even keep myself together at the damn dinner table in front of his mother, for fuck's sake.

The rest of the dinner was just miserable. I tried to be invisible, but since they could smell me, I may as well have danced on the table. My relief may have been visible when Callum said our goodnights. I don't care. We are both quiet as we walk up the stairs and into the room I have been assigned. I am more than a little nervous when he turns and shuts the door, locks it, and places a chair under the handle. Then, he says, "This won't stop a vampire coming in your room, but it will stop them being quiet about it."

He looks so serious, and I can't help it. The laughter just bubbles up and out. He is in front of me in less than a heartbeat. "So you can laugh. I like the sound. I must find more ways to inspire laughter from you."

The room feels suddenly very small and lacks breathable air. I don't need it so much anymore, but breathing is still a habit, and I feel like I can't do so much. I need to keep in mind I am nothing to him. Nothing. Things will be easier once I am home with Blair and Duncan. For now, I take a shaky breath and a step back, only to run into my bed. Of course. He steps forward, pinning me between him and the bed as he breathes in deeply. "I make you nervous. And hot." He inhales next to my ear. "I will be in the next room, reading something completely riveting, so I don't come back here and give you exactly what your body says you want. If you should need me, for anything, simply call out. I will… come… to your aid."

He inhales one more time and pushes himself away. I watch as he walks over to the connecting door while muttering about cold showers. He leaves the door partially open and, while I would prefer privacy, I feel safer knowing that he can hear everything in here in case of attack.

Chapter Eleven

Callum

The message from Diane feels wrong. Looking at Olivia, I tell her, "I need to speak to Diane. I will return in a few minutes. Shout if anyone bothers you."

She nods as she takes a bite of her breakfast. Before I leave, she has her phone out, and a book pulled up, propping the phone against her untouched ice water glass. I asked her why she never drinks the water when I first noticed it. She looked at me like I was dumb and said 'it's bad for the digestion.' I did not know. I don't know if it is really something a vampire has to concern themselves with, but it's important to her. Once we leave the family estate, I'll ensure that she doesn't have to worry about that anymore. Diane is in her office, looking for new ways to start shit, I'm sure. I walk in without knocking and she jumps. I am even more suspicious.

"What game are you playing? There is no reason why I need to go sign this contract."

"They requested you. And you are here. Go represent the

family. Your little girlfriend will be fine here, while you tend to the contract. Go do your family duty.”

“Fine. I will be taking her with me, Mother.”

“No,” she near shouts at me as I turn to leave. “You will not take a family member new to this world to a signing this important. You know, as well as I do, that the slightest misstep could ruin everything. Leave her here.”

I have a terrible feeling about this. But she isn’t wrong. One wrong look could cancel the contract entirely and cause a small war that we can ill afford while we are so divided. “If you so much as touch a hair on her head, I will destroy everything you hold dear.”

“Yes, all the torment if she is injured. Go. I don’t have time for your dramatics.”

Deciding to ignore the baiting comment, I leave her office and go back to Olivia. She is eating slowly as she reads. Stopping in the doorway, I lean against the frame to watch her. Her hair is in a braid, mussed from sleeping. She wears a tank top and pajama bottoms that have little daggers printed all over them. She is adorable. I could watch her for hours.

“Olivia.” Her eyes never stop moving, and I know she isn’t aware of the rest of the world. Walking around the table, I pull out the chair next to her and sit.

She turns to me. “Oh, that didn’t take very long at all.”

“No, however, I’m afraid I need to escort you back to your room. Mother insists that I be the one to handle the signing of this contract, and I don’t have a way to refuse this.”

She nods and stands, grabbing her phone as she does. Her movement gifts me a very close view of the curves of her hips and ass. I just want to grab those hips and press her body to mine. I don’t have time for that right now, but gods, she is tempting. We walk back to her room arm in arm, still pretending to be much closer than she will allow me.

I know she doesn't want us to be close for reasons she can't trust me with. It feeds a part of my soul that I didn't know starved to have her close like this. All too soon, we are back in her room. I wedge a chair under her door and lock it. She watches, mildly amused.

Crossing the room, I stop just inches away from her. "I need you to stay in this room until I return. No matter what. Stay here. Promise me you will stay here."

She looks up at me, and I see the brat side of her wants to deny my request, just because. She bites her lower lip, and all I can think about is kissing those lips. "Yes. I will stay in here. But only because I trust everyone out there way less than you. Don't get any big ideas about me being good and obedient."

I can't help but chuckle at her. "No, I would never presume to such a thing. I want to keep you safe, and this is the option. May I have a kiss before I go?"

She smiles and looks away. "I suppose one, little kiss wouldn't kill me."

She turns her face up to mine, and I lean down, pressing my lips to hers. I meant to have a single kiss, but the electricity of the connection went through us both, and her lips parted under mine. Next thing I know, she is in my arms and giving as good as she is getting.

Then, she puts her hands on my chest and breaks the kiss. She breathes hard as she says, "You should go. You have contracts to sign."

A growl rumbles up from my chest. "I'm going, but I would much rather stay here and kiss you out of these clothes."

I release her, and she steps back. "Go. I don't need this

complication right now. I will stay here in this room while you are gone."

"Thank you. I will return as quickly as I can."

OLIVIA

Admittedly, when Callum asked me to stay in these rooms, I almost walked out the door right then. But I held back, though, and made the mistake of letting him kiss me. I should never have allowed it. I am nothing to him. But he was so charming this morning and so sweet when he asked for a kiss.

I wasn't expecting the electricity that ran through my body when our lips touched. Or the passion with which I returned the kiss. I can't even really blame him for that. I was just as much at fault.

With him gone, I lounge in the chair to finish reading this book. Which I was happily doing, until I heard the knock at my door. I wonder if I should stay still and pretend I am not here? Waiting, I hold my breath and keep still. The person on the other side of the door walks away, only to open the door to Callum's bedroom and walk through to the door between our rooms.

"Why did you not answer when I knocked?"

"I am not required to answer my door just because someone taps on it. What are you doing by walking into Callum's room like it was your own?"

The man hisses at me, and I just raise my brows at him. Men are so easily offended. It's like they walk around looking for a reason to be upset.

His face falls back into the civilized veneer the entire

family wears, and he says, "Diane requests your presence in her study."

"I will attend to her as soon as Callum returns. He told me to stay in my rooms until then. Tell her she might take that point of contention up with her son."

"You misunderstand. The mistress' request is an order to be obeyed. And you will, one way or," he smiles evilly, "another."

"I see. Then, you will wait outside our rooms while I ready myself."

"I see no reason to leave for that."

"You will leave while I ready myself, or I will tell the world how you attempted to force yourself on one of the Mezzasalma family. What do you think your mistress will do about someone bringing shame to her table? She doesn't seem the lenient type. But you know her better than I do. What do you suppose her reaction will be, if I assume wrong?"

The man glares at me. "I will be outside, do not tarry."

He walks across the room and kicks the chair away from the door. There is a loud crack when it lands. I think it is not going to be something they can repair after this. He turns the knob viciously, breaking the locking mechanism with an awful sound. Callum was right. It won't stop a vampire, but it does stop them from being quiet. I hope those pieces will remain as evidence, if something happens to me.

Once he is out, I hop up and run to my dresser. I have paper and pencil there. My handwriting is shit when I am scared like this. Hopefully, Callum can read it. Looking around, I don't know where I should put it. I settle for shoving it partially under a tray. My pajamas are not fit for the head of the family, but I don't know what I have that would be.

Really, she is just a bitch on a power trip. I never would have had these concerns at Roman's house. But I'm not at Roman's house. I'm in this shit place, and I have to pretend I give a shit about what she thinks about me. I've wasted too much time.

Grabbing a pair of slacks and a blouse, I dash off to the bathroom and change as fast as possible. Coming back out, I grab my phone and slide my feet into a pair of flats. A breath to steady my head, and I walk out into the hall. That odious man waits for me, as promised. He turns on his heel and strides off, leaving me to keep up as I can. Unfortunately for him, I have no problem following him to what feels like my doom.

Her study door is before us far too soon, and he opens it after a tap. I have a feeling I am stepping into my own, personal hell as I walk through the doorway. "You requested my presence?"

Diane smirks, "I did, sit. We'll have tea."

Having no other choice, I seat myself in the chair across from her. A low table with a tea service is all that separates me from this woman that has hated me since I arrived. I watch as she pours us both tea. My eyes don't miss the powder that quickly dissolves in the cup she hands me. Callum's warning flashes through my head, and I know now that she is fully aware of what people say about her. Everyone around her plays checkers while she dominates chess, and I am in deeper shit than I thought. She picks up her cup and sips. I do the same, except I don't allow the liquid to touch my lips.

Diane says, "I would like to know you better, while it is just us girls. Tell me about your childhood."

The cup and saucer feel like lead weights in my hands as I tell her, "There isn't much to tell. I was a child, and I grew up. My parents were nothing special, not good or bad."

"I see. When you met my Callum? Was it terribly romantic?"

"I don't remember much," that I would reveal to you. "Most of that night was a blur."

She sips her tea again and watches as I pretend to sip mine. A second later, she rings a bell that I had not noticed next to her. Two of the larger men I've seen following her around enter the room from a door behind her. "Since you are not drinking the tea and cooperating, you can go sit in my dungeon until I decide what I want to do with you."

I nod. I really am somewhat relieved. Now I know what is coming. I'll never see my Nims again because I am going to die down in her dungeon. I look at the tea in my hands, and some feral part of me takes over. I watch in horror, mixed with fierce joy, as the hand holding the cup moves and throws the poisoned tea directly at Diane. It hits her face and drips down onto her blouse and lap, smoking and sizzling. The flesh on her face blisters, but she seems to be healing fast. One of the men slaps me, nearly knocking me out of the chair.

She never moves as her face and neck heal. Standing, I turn from her and walk around the chair to where the men wait. "Shall we? I really hate being in the company of bitches."

My face is slapped again, but I don't care. One man leads the way, and the other follows behind me as we leave the room.

Chapter Twelve

Olivia

The basement is dark and smells musty. Doesn't that just figure? I can finally walk in the sunlight, and I am about to be locked in a dungeon before I even really enjoy it. I can't help but chuckle at the irony of it all. The men on either side of me both look at me like I've lost my mind.

They are probably right. One shoves me into the cage. They had the door open and waiting just for me. The door clangs shut, and the sound is loud in the oppressive silence of what will probably be my tomb.

I watch them leave, and they close a thick door I hadn't noticed. The darkness isn't scary by itself. I wonder if they will wait until I am nothing but bones to come and collect before they open that door again?

As my eyes adjust, I see small slivers of light through the ceiling. I wonder what room this is under? My throat feels tight with the urge to scream, but I'm afraid that if I start, I won't ever stop.

I remember my phone in my pocket and pull it out. When the display lights up, it shows I have maybe half a bar of signal. Shit. I don't know that Callum isn't a part of this. If I can get a message out, I'm sure as hell not sending it to one of my would-be jailors.

Maybe he just didn't want to have the embarrassment of a nothing being brought into the family by him. Duncan would start a war, and I need him to keep Nims safe. Blair, though, he would talk to the witches. If I can get enough signal to send one message to him.

Its got to be just one word, the least amount of data to be sent. I'll just send the word help and hope like hell they can figure it out before I die. Before Nims dies without me. What is she going to do when I don't call tomorrow? It feels like my heart is being crushed, and the scream becomes harder to hold back.

I tap out my message to Blair and hit send. I see a small ledge made from a stone sticking out a little further than the rest. Grabbing one of the bars and bracing a foot against it, I manage to leverage myself high enough to set the phone on it. I can only hope it will find enough signal to blast the message to Blair. And that he gets here in time. For Nims' sake, if nothing else.

CALLUM

The signing took entirely too long. I soon realized they were being intentionally slow, but there was nothing I could do beyond pretending it didn't matter.

I don't know if they believed me, but it was hours before I could leave. Once I am home, the house is ominously quiet. Running, I go straight for her room. The door is standing open with a new knob. I can smell the fresh oil in it. What I can't smell is Olivia. Reaching out, I push the door further open. The room looks as though she had never been there. Even the scent of her has been erased.

Rage builds as I realize this is Diane's doing. Spinning around, I head for her favorite haunts. When I finally catch her scent, she is in what she calls the atrium, but there isn't a single fucking plant in it. It has a lot of windows and is a large, open space with various seating arrangements.

She looks up when I walk in. "Callum, did the signing not go well?"

"The signing went fine. What did you do with her?"

She looks away, as if she is reluctant to say anything. In a flash I am in front of her, her throat in my hand, "No thinking up a story. Answer me now. Where. is. Olivia."

She frowns and nods, so I ease the pressure on her throat. "I helped her escape."

"Escape from what?"

Her mask of sorrow, feigned or real, looks up at me. I've never been able to tell which mask was the truth with her. "She was trying to escape you, Callum."

With those seven words, my world crashed around me. My heart froze in my chest. Why? I was taking her home. She didn't need to escape from me. Releasing Diane, I turn and leave the room. She says something, but I'm not listening. Up the stairs and into my room. Diane's favorite butler comes in, hot on my trail. "Madame was not done speaking with you."

"I am done speaking with her. Leave, or I will put you out the window for my troubles."

"You wouldn't dare."

His insolence strikes a cord, and before I think about it, I pick him up by the collar of his shirt and the waist of his pants. He shouts for me 'to put him down this instant' as he watches the carpet go by. Just a few quick steps, and I am in front of the window. He is screaming now, high-pitched and shrill, as I swing him back and then throw him through the window. Glass explodes outward as he crashes through. I lean out and watch him fall, watch as he hits the cobblestone patio below.

He is moving almost immediately after he hits. Moving slowly and painfully as he works himself to a standing position. He looks up and sees me watching. He raises one arm and extends his middle finger toward me.

I don't care. He'll think twice before forcing his presence on me again.

Chapter Thirteen

I haven't been able to get Olivia out of my mind since the first day I met her. Seeing her wandering in with Nims, and her delight over the food we have available. Olivia was joy embodied, and all I could think was that I must talk with her, if she will allow it.

It's taken years for me to get past that wall she uses to keep the world from hurting her. I'd love to turn Callum into kibble for Nims as repayment for his snatching her from us. The fucker.

My phone pings, and I see a message from Olivia. Smiling doesn't last too long as I open it, and my heart stops.

Help.

Tapping the screen, I call her phone. It goes straight to voicemail. Panic sets in, hard and fast. I don't even know where she is. How do I find her? Go to Italy and start wandering the place, looking for her scent? She could be dead by the time I find her. How do I—the witches! Yes!

I start to head for the door, patting myself as I go, making sure I have keys, phone to show the message to the witches, shoes on my feet. Is there anything else? Fuck it, I don't need anything here right now. The door slams behind me as I take off running to their shop.

Moments later, I skid to a stop just inside the store. Looking at the witch behind the counter, I ask, "Where's Ailsa? I need to see her right now. It's about Olivia!"

The witch looked annoyed until I said Olivia. Then, her eyes widened, and she looked at the door to the back room. Turning back to me, she says, "She'll see you immediately."

She leads me through and directly to Ailsa's office, leaving me there. I walk in and close the door behind me. As I turn to face the interior, I realize that I am not in her office after all. This looks like a living room. I hear her call out, "In here, Blair. Old witches take longer to wake up, and we need our coffee. What's wrong with Olivia?"

Following the sound of her voice, I find her in the kitchen, sipping coffee at her table. Instead of telling her, I pull out my phone and bring up the message, handing it over for her to see. She reads it once, twice, and then, her coffee falls from her hands, hitting the table and splashing divine liquid everywhere.

Ailsa stands, and she waves a hand while whispering something I can't quite make out. I feel a coolness wash over me. She says, "I have put a protection on you. The vampires will not be able to do harm to you. You are going to her now. She is in the Chiogga region of Italy." A piece of paper appears in her hand, and she passes it to me. "This is the address. Go to her and demand to see her. Do not take no for an answer. The Mezzasalma will not be able to touch you, with the exception of Olivia. She is in that castle. Tear it down to the foundation, if you need to, but find Olivia. If you run into trouble you cannot handle, say my name. I will be there. It would be better if I do not go. Diane is no friend of mine. Do not trust her." She waves her hand, and my suitcase lands with a thunk next to me. "Go. Directly to the airport. Your ticket will be waiting by the time you arrive." I open my mouth to ask where I should start looking, and she says, "That isn't important. It will become clear when you arrive. Go. Now."

Well, I guess she isn't answering questions. Grabbing my suitcase, I head to the door I came in, which looked to be the front door. Opening it, I step through and find myself at the airport. Walking out of the men's room. Holy shit. I check my suitcase because I certainly didn't have any identification with me when I left. My wallet and passport are tucked in the side pocket.

The witches are amazing and a little scary. Ailsa especially. I head for the ticket desk, pulling out the phone that is back in my pocket, even though I distinctly recall Ailsa holding it as I left. I send a quick text to Mom, letting her know I can't be at the shop for the next little while.

Chapter Fourteen

BLAIR

Two fucking days. Two days to get from the airport to this shit estate. The entire country seems intent on keeping me from there without an invitation. Fuckers. The witch driving me takes one look at me and says, "The destination you entered on the app isn't where you are going."

"No. I need to go to the Mezzasalma Estate. I was sent by Ailsa. Will you please take me there?"

She chuckles, "Yes. This is why they sent me. They must have hoped I would dispose of you for being so difficult. Get in. I can see Ailsa's magic all over you."

No sooner than I lift my foot from the ground as I sit in the car, she takes off. I hurry to shut the door. She doesn't seem to notice as she steers us out of the city at speeds that give even me a little anxiety.

The countryside is a blur as she drives. It feels like she is using magic to move us much faster and with no obstructions. I don't care, so long as it gets me to Olivia. She slams on the brakes, and the car screeches to a stop in the driveway of the Mezzasalma Estate. I pull out some cash and hand it to her.

"Thanks for bringing me. I'll give you five stars in the app. Here's extra for making it faster than it could have been. I appreciate it, and I will make sure Ailsa knows you helped me. What is your name?"

"Chiara. Here," she extends her hand, and a card materializes between her fingers. "Take this. Message me if you need a ride anywhere in Italy. I will be your only driver here. You will get where you are going."

I take the card from where it perched on her finger very gently, "Thank you. I really appreciate this."

She shrugs. "Go. I have work to do."

The car takes off as I swing the door closed. Turning, I look at the damn castle before me. I sure do hope I don't have to tear this thing down.

I knock on the door and wait. No one answers. I can hear people walking past the door. Assholes. I pound on it like the damn thing offended me. The door opens moments later, and a self-important stuffed shirt opens the door and says, "Why are you here?"

Shoving down the urge to give him a lesson on manners, I tell him, "I need to see Callum."

"He's not available to you."

The stuffed shirt swings the door to close, and I put out a hand, stopping it. "You misunderstand me, friend. I didn't ask to see him. Either you bring Callum to me, or I can wander the halls, wrecking shit till I find him. Your choice, friend."

The stuffed shirt reaches for my arm and his fingers crumple as he hits the witch's protections on me. He shouts with pain and rage, then he whimpers a bit as he pulls his fingers back into place.

"Terrible when they heal in the wrong place, eh? Before we make more rash moves, how about we think it through? I've got protections, obviously. Maybe it would be better to let me wait in a room while someone fetches Callum for me, eh?"

The stuffed shirt's lips, thin as they were, have disappeared entirely. His face reveals nothing beyond the disappearance of his lips. "This way. You may wait in the receiving room."

Following stuffed shirt is an exercise in patience. He walks with measured, short steps. But, we get to a room where he opens the door and says, "Please wait here. Callum will be with you soon."

"Excellent, friend." I clap a hand on his back to let him know I can touch him. Looking him in the eye, I tell him, "I'm sure he'll be in here before I start destroying the place in five minutes."

His eye twitches, and he nods as he turns away and starts walking toward the big-ass staircase. Walking into the room, I find it is fairly nice. There are some chairs and low tables. I would guess this is the room for unwanted guests or guests of very low standing. Being a wolf shifter, I am really low on their list for prestige. I don't care, though. I'm here for Olivia.

I can smell that she was in this house recently. The scent of her would have faded, if she wasn't somewhere inside. Footsteps sound behind me. I know Callum chose to make noise as he walked. I turn to face him. "Where is she?"

His face goes through a gamut of emotions before he schools it and says, "My mother helped her to run away because she was afraid of me. I don't know where she is."

"Wrong. She sent me a text two days ago with one word. Help. Her phone has been unreachable since. The witches sent me to find her. Will you help me, or do I start tearing this place down to the foundations?"

His uncaring front drops, and his mouth falls open. I watch as things click in his head, and his mouth snaps shut, a muscle twitching in his jaw. He shuts the door and starts pacing. "We won't find any help from anyone here. They are all afraid of Mother."

"I can smell her. I know she is here somewhere."

"You can? I thought her scent was just lingering to torment me. If you can track her down that way, fetch. Let's go." A growl erupts from my throat when he says fetch. He smiles, "Isn't finding her right now much more important than punishing me for snark?"

"Watch your step, vampire." He opens the door, and I step past him. Out in the open area, I walk toward the middle of the room. I turn a slow circle, sniffing the air. I catch a slightly stronger whiff of her. As I walk toward the scent, Callum stays in step with me. His face gets sharper as I head down a hall. I almost pass the staircase, but the scent of her starts to fade, and I make the turn to go into the darkness. Callum is behind me. The stairway is narrow and old. The air coming up from below smells dank. A vampire appears out of the darkness in front of me. "You may not come down here. Who let you in here, wolf?"

Callum's hand flashes past my shoulder and hits the man, sending him crashing backward down the stairs. He says, "I should go handle that. Mind if I slide past you?"

"Not at all." I turn to back myself against the wall, and Callum puts his back against the wall I am facing. He is past me and down the stairs in a flash. I hear a scuffle as I follow at a slower pace. When I get down the stairs, he is finishing a meal. He drops the other vampire to the dirty floor and says, "After you."

Stepping over the vampire, I follow Olivia's scent further into the darkness. It becomes stronger till I reach a locked door. "She is on the other side of this door. Do you have the key or shall I open it the old-fashioned way?"

"Wait. This is the room that Mother puts people in to forget about. Olivia is going to be bad off. No bright lights, and allow me to open it for you."

I step back, and he snatches the door open. I hear a scuffle in the darkness. Callum lights up the display on his phone and turns it toward the sound. Olivia is hunkered in a corner of the cage. Her hands are clapped tightly over her ears, and her eyes scrunched closed. I can see her lips moving, but no sound is coming out of her mouth.

I walk over to the cage and give the door a yank. It moves a fraction of an inch. Looking back at Callum, I say, "Give me a hand with this?"

He stares at her, horrified. What I said registers, and he shoves his phone in his pocket. Coming over to stand next to me, he puts his hands on the bars. "On three. One, two, three!" We heave the door, and it moves out another inch. "One more time should do it," I tell him. "On three."

The door gives way this time, with a screech of metal on metal.

Chapter Fifteen

OLIVIA

I hear noises and see shapes moving in the dark again. The first time it happened, I nearly killed myself trying to reach them. But no one is coming for me. My message never went out. No one knows where I am. And no one here cares. They left me here to die.

The noises are persistent this time, I can't take it. I back away from the sounds till I am against a corner. My mind plays tricks on me. Why? I feel the tears flow down my face as I cover my ears. Crouching down in the corner with my eyes shut, I whisper to myself, "Not real, not real, not real."

I can't let myself believe someone is here for me.

Suddenly, I am scooped up against a warm chest. I would swear it smells like Blair. But that can't be? Then, he whispers, "You're okay, I got you. I promise, I am as real as you. I've got you, Olivia, and I am never letting you go."

The tears flow harder as I open my eyes and I see his face. Wrapping my arms around him, the sobs are loud and ugly, but I don't care as I try to tell him, "I—didn't—the message—it got through."

"Shh, it got through. Let's get you out of here."

"Wait! My phone. I need it! It got the message out. I can't leave it in the dark, alone!" The panic welling up in me stopped the sobs, but I have to get my phone. I start wiggling to get down, and Blair's arms clamp down, effectively shutting off my struggle as weak as I am.

His chest rumbles, and he says, "Callum will make himself useful fetching the phone. You stay right here. Where will he find it?"

"In the corner, toward the front of the cell. There is a ledge up near the top."

I hear steps and see the soft glow of a light point up toward my phone. I watch as Callum's hand stretches up and closes around my phone. He turns and brings it to me. My hands reach for the phone as though it were my lifeline. Phone safely in my hands, I say, "I can't believe you came. I thought you didn't care. That I was nothing to you." Before he can answer, Blair starts walking. I ask him, "Is my Nims all right? Have you seen her recently? I couldn't get in touch with her. Do you think I could call her, when we are where there is a signal? Before anything else happens?"

"Of course, you can call her. When were you put down there?"

"Right after they sent Callum away. I'm not sure how long that is."

Callum swears, "Son of a bitch. It's been four days. She's too young to go so long."

Blair says, "Then, she'll have mine."

He lifts me toward that beautiful vein pulsing in his throat, but Callum stops him, saying, "She might drain you dry and still be starved. Let her feed on me while you hold her. Please."

"Very well." He lowers me away, and Callum puts his

wrist before me. I am starving. I want to tear into it. It takes so much energy to be slow and methodical.

Bringing his wrist to my mouth, I bite into him. Feeling the sweet rush of life-giving blood fill my mouth and my belly. Callum smooths my hair back. "Drink, my precious little one. Drink and grow strong. We'll make sure nothing like this ever happens to you again. Even if I have to murder the entire family to ensure it." Once my thirst is calmed, I release his wrist. He looks a little surprised, then he says, "Let's get her to the rooms, and you can stay with her while I get her some more blood."

Blair nods, and the two of them start walking. That shady fucking butler is carrying a tray down the hall when he sees us. His mouth falls open, and he drops the tray, dishes, and teapot. The items break and clang as he stands there. He watches like he is seeing a ghost, so I lift a hand and put up my middle finger, making sure to lift it, so he knows it's for him. Then, we are past him, and Callum is holding the door open as Blair walks me into my room.

That nasty butler comes stomping up to the door, putting a hand flat on it to stop Callum from closing it. Blair finishes setting me on the bed and faces them. Callum's tongue presses on his canine tooth, the sharpness slicing it. He seems to be a little less frayed as he says, "You should leave, Graham."

Graham puffs up. "She is not to be here. Madam said she is banned from the house, and should she show up, she is to be thrown in the dungeon."

Callum rolls his shoulders. "Blair, you'll guard her?"

Blair growls, "I will. And if he thinks he will get anywhere near her, I'll feed his blood to her myself."

Graham looks a little less confident, and then he is fighting for his life as Callum has him by the throat and walks him out of the room on his toes. Blair snorts, walks over and closes the door to the hall, followed by the door to Callum's room. Once he is done, he walks over and sits on the edge of the bed. "Does your phone have any charge left?"

I tap the screen, and nothing happens. "No."

He pulls his phone out of his pocket, taps the screen a few times and shifts around to sit next to me, with the camera pointed at both of us.

Duncan answers and says, "Oh, thank fuck! Olivia, what happened to you? Are you all right? Blair, who did this to her? When are you all coming home?"

Blair answers before I can. "As soon as she can handle the flight home. The Mezzasalmas and the vampire courts can all suck my dick about it. She isn't staying here."

Duncan nods, "Good. Olivia, what happened to you?"

"I was put in a cell and left to die." Nims cries loudly, and my heart breaks for her. "Let me see her!" Before I finish, Duncan is knocked to the floor, and he points the phone at Nims. "Oh, my little love! I miss you so much. I'm coming home to you. I promise. I am coming home to you as soon as I can."

She cries a little more and makes noises at me to tell me she loves me and misses me. She looks thin. I wonder if she hasn't been eating. "I'll be there as soon as I can. You make sure you eat. I need you to be healthy when I get there. We'll spend a week or three in the house. You, me and the doggos. We'll do our routines, just us." She howls and taps her feet. Judging by the grunts, she is stomping on Duncan. "All right, love, let him up. I'll talk to you again tonight. Blair is here to make sure I can."

She growls and grumbles while looking toward Blair. He chuckles. "I know. I won't leave her side, and I am bringing her home to you."

Nims nods and makes her I love you noises at me. "I love you, too, Nims. I'm lost without you." She steps off Duncan, and he turns the phone to face himself.

"So, you'll be home soon?"

"Yes," Blair and I both answer at the same time. I chuckle and say, "Yes. I am coming home as soon as I possibly can. If you hadn't guessed, I've had enough of this place, and the vampire courts can suck my dick, too."

"Well, that's… That's a picture. Ok, then. Blair, keep me updated on the travel plans, and I will talk to you both this evening. Hopefully, not from the floor."

Callum steps forward from the doorway and brings me a couple bags of blood. I bite into one, drinking slowly. I seem to remember something from being human that if you eat too fast or drink too fast after not having anything for a while, it could make you sick. I don't know if it applies to vampires or not. Blair lifts me and slides me over on the bed a little, then seats himself and puts an arm around me. I snuggle into him as I drink. My eyelids are so heavy.

CALLUM

I watch her as she falls asleep, blood bag still in her mouth. Once she is asleep, Blair gently takes the bag from her and settles himself to stay. I take the bag from him and deposit it in the garbage. I never realized I could feel this level of rage over another person.

Looking at Blair, I ask, "Is there a type of food you don't like?"

Blair looks suspicious but replies, "Not fond of beets. Everything else is game, though."

"I am ordering food. I need to take care of something. I

will return when the food arrives. Do not take food from anyone else. If I do not return, leave with her when she wakes. You'll find keys to my cars hanging on the wall in my bedroom."

He nods. "Fuck'em up. I got her."

I call a place in town as I leave the room, closing the door behind me. They answer in Italian, and I reply in that language. It rolls off my tongue, feeling a bit like coming home after so long speaking English. When I finish, I have ordered about half the main dishes on the menu and an assortment of appetizers. Just as I end the call, I see Diane walking through the open area. She looks like she is on a mission.

Running across the room, I snatch her up by the throat and slam her to the floor. She growls and tries to escape, stilling and trying to look friendly when that doesn't work. "Callum, what are you playing at? Are you still distraught over your pet leaving you?"

"Distraught? No, Mother, you overplayed your hand. I have Olivia back in my custody. You will toe the fucking line, or I will put the door back on that fucking cage and leave you to the faint hope that Father will release you before you starve to death. Very faint hope for you, as we both know he can't stand you. You are a matriarch at the moment, but that can be changed. In fact, let's call my father."

I pull my phone out of my pocket, and she struggles again. I lift her a little and smack her back onto the floor. Tiles crack under her, but I don't care. A few taps with my thumb, and a call is going through. I hit the button to put it on speaker in time for him to answer. "Hello, Callum, what can I do for you?"

"I'm holding your wife to the floor by her throat. She has

tried to murder my protégé." I give him the short version of recent events, and how the witches are very involved.

"Can Diane hear me?"

"Yes, she can."

"Good. You have broken our agreement. You will go wait in your room until I return, or renounce the marriage and your position as you leave my home. What is your decision?"

She is glaring at me as she says, "I will await you in my room."

"Do not leave it once you are in there. You will take your meals in there. Not even so much as a toenail in the hall. My people will be there in the morning to ensure my orders are followed. Son, let her go to her room." I release her, and she stands, walking slowly toward the stairs as demanded. I tap the icon on the screen of my phone to make it a private call again. Father asks, "Has she left the room?"

"Yes, though slowly."

"I'll keep that in mind. The girl, will she be all right? How long was she down there?"

"She will be better soon. I need to take her away from here. I am uncertain that I will be able to keep from tearing your wife into tiny bits, if I stay. Olivia was trapped in that cage for four days. She is barely a decade old."

"I see. Make an announcement of your mother's disgrace and see that it goes out to everyone. Wait until my enforcers arrive in the morning, and then you may take her elsewhere. You will continue her training and making her a credit to our name."

"Yes, I will continue her training. She is already a credit to the name."

Chapter Sixteen

Olivia

It is dark and quiet where I am. I feel safe and comfortable finally. Except for one thing, one thing that will not allow me to continue to sink deeper into the sweet darkness. My stomach is empty and rumbling. Trying to eat itself to get me to notice it and wake up. I want to cry knowing that food is not coming, but then I remember Blair is here. Callum is here. They found me. I let my eyes open slowly, and I find I am laying in my bed at the family estate. Blair is next to me on one side, and Callum on the other. Blair leans over so his face is in my field of vision. "Hey there. Now that you are awake, want some food?"

No sooner than the words leave his mouth, I smell it. It smells like carb heaven. "Yes, please. I'm starving."

"Good. Sit up, I'll get you a variety plate, and you can eat what you like."

Fear, sharp and close, pierces my heart. "Wait. She didn't —Diane hasn't touched the food, has she?"

Callum answers, "No. I ordered it to be delivered from in town, and I waited downstairs for it to arrive."

"I suppose it is ok, then. You're sure she hasn't been near it?"

Callum nods as I struggle into an upright position. He watches, and I can tell he is refraining from helping me. Eventually, he can't resist, and he grabs pillows to put behind me. He brushes my hair away from my face, telling me, "Diane is imprisoned within her bedroom by order of my father."

"How? Why?"

"Their marriage was only ever about political gain. He allowed her to do as she pleased, so long as it was beneficial to the family. He could understand why she felt killing him might align with that thought. However, the first vampire added to our family in over a hundred years? One that is being claimed by another vampire family and is, therefore, obviously much more valuable to our family? That is not good for this family by any stretch. It gives my father the upper hand, as she has broken the marriage contract."

"How did your father find out?"

Callum's tongue presses on the point of his tooth as he smiles. "I called him as I held Diane on the floor by her throat. Unfortunately, that does mean she is aware of how important you are. I hope you will forgive me, as it makes you more of a target."

"You wanted her to think you didn't care to protect me?"

"Of course. What other reason would there be?"

That you didn't care at all. I am saved from having to say anything by Blair. He hands me a plate piled high with food, saying, "Here you go. Eat as much as you like. Callum tried to buy out the restaurant and has a lot of what appears to be every dish they serve."

Callum turns serious as he says, "Our vampire ball was postponed. Diane wanted me to attend, and I refused, so she had rescheduled it for tonight and had commanded that I make an appearance. As she is imprisoned in her room, and my father's enforcers will be here by morning to ensure that no one gets complacent about keeping her in there, I am responsible for hosting tonight. You should attend. The problem is, only vampires are allowed."

Blair interjects, "And the witches were very clear that I am to stay by her side, no matter what."

"Yes. And there is the dilemma."

A terrible thought occurs to me, and a giggle escapes my lips before I can stop it. The two of them look at me, and I can see the question in their eyes. "Blair, this is just an intrusive thought. Really. I just thought, what if he goes in his wolf form? Everyone would take him for a giant dog." Blair scowls as Callum laughs hard. I look at Blair. "It would work. You know, most vampires are pretty full of themselves. Even if they thought you smelled like a wolf, they would convince themselves that I had somehow tamed a wild creature before they would be able to accept the idea that a shifter was at their ball. Guarding one of them from them."

Blair growls at me, terribly scary that one. Though, if I weren't so tired, that growl would do things to me. Callum's laughter fades away, and he says, "You know, that could actually work. Dogs are so rare in our world because of their short life spans. Any time one is brought out, everyone gets excited and wants to pet the dog."

Blair grits out, "I bite."

"Yes, I know. Werewolf, scary, bite. Got it. And she can tell people that you aren't friendly. This way, you will be right there to protect her. You can watch everyone in ways that I cannot. That she cannot. You know how vampire society is. Plus, she won't have to stay long. It is readily obvious that Olivia is not ok just yet. Her presence downstairs will be noticed, remarked upon, and questioned as they study her. We will spend the time that she is there telling everyone of what Diane did. That will garner support for what my father does when he arrives."

Blair is still shaking his head no when I lay one of my hands on his. He looks down at it, and my eyes follow his. I see how my fingers are nearly skeletal in appearance. As though the flesh were draped over my bones, no muscles or tissue of any kind between them and skin. "Please do this. I want Diane to suffer. I want her to feel some small amount of what I felt in that cage. Will you do this for me?"

He frowns and nods. "I will. But I'm not going to like it. And those vampires better keep their hands to themselves."

Callum smiles a little too wide as he says, "She can just tell them you get a little carried away with the biting. Everyone knows it takes for-fucking-ever to grow back an arm."

Chapter Seventeen

BLAIR

There are bloodsuckers everywhere. Callum's father's enforcers have arrived early and are currently upstairs with Diane. Judging by the shrieking earlier, she was not pleased to see them. At least, I get to be in my wolf form around all of them. Too many unknowns for my comfort. This place, these vampires. They are nothing like the ones Roman rules. Olivia is not as recovered as I would prefer to be around these people. Treachery and violence are so thick in the air, I can barely breathe.

Olivia is talking to a woman, and she starts to reach out to pet me. But when she looks over and sees me, she jerks her hand back and seems a little more shattered. Oh fuck, I know why. Nims and I have the same coloring, though our resemblance ends there. Thank the gods we are leaving for home in the morning. I don't know that she could survive much longer.

Another woman comes up and asks to pet me as she reaches for my face. I growl as Olivia quickly sets her hand on my head and tells the woman, "No, you don't want to touch him. He bites, and I am told it takes a very long time to regrow an arm."

Callum walks over, smirks at me with something clutched in his hand. He presents it to Olivia. "I didn't want your dog to feel left out. I got him a bow tie. Look, it has diamond accents."

Olivia holds it up, and I growl at Callum as she studies it. He chuckles as she says, "It's so cute! He will be dashing in it." Son of a bitch. I have to let her put it on me. She kneels down in front of me. "Blair, darling, can I put this on you?" Sighing, I shake my head yes for her. As she clips it around my neck, I glare up at Callum. He is entirely too cheerful about this. Maybe I'll bite him when I get the chance. She is done and is now telling me how handsome I am. That wipes the smile right off his face.

An hour passes, and Olivia is looking tired. Vampires aren't supposed to get tired. I let a high-pitched whine out, and her focus and back sling off whoever she was telling her story to this time in exchange for me. I whimper for her a few more times, and she nods. Standing back up, she faces the person she was talking to. "I'm sorry. I have to go. My puppy isn't used to being out so late. You understand. I hope to speak with you again in the future."

She barely finishes speaking and I have my head under her hand, guiding her to the stairs. She glides along beside me, never even glancing back at the vampires we are leaving behind. Something doesn't seem right. As soon as we clear the bedroom door, I shift and turn to face her. Just in time to catch her as her strength gives out. Laying her on the bed, I don't know what to do. I've never had a vampire collapse on me before.

Maybe blood will bring her around? Fuck, it can't hurt to try. Slicing across my arm, I hold it over her mouth. Nothing happens for long seconds as the blood drips past her lips. Slowly a hand comes up, and she touches my arm, and she drinks. Even so, she isn't trying to drain me. Her drinking is light, almost as though she is determined not to take any more than she must. She releases my arm and sighs. "Thank you. I haven't been hungry all the time like this since I was newly turned."

"What's a little blood between lovers? Are you sure you don't need more? It doesn't seem like you took much at all."

She shakes her head, "No. I'll be fine. It was just a lot talking to so many people. I think, I think I need some sleep. Will you be here?"

"I will. You're safe. Sleep. Tomorrow we'll get you home, get you to Nims."

She whispers, "I'll see her in my dreams. We're always together there."

My heart breaks for her. I have a terrible feeling though, like something just isn't right, and I don't know what it is. Pulling out my phone, I tap the screen a few times. Duncan answers before it even rings, "Is she okay?"

"I'm not sure. How does Nims look?"

"Like Olivia has been gone too long. She eats what I make her eat and no more. She just went to sleep."

The bad feeling intensifies. "You know what? We'll be home in a few hours. I'll get more information for you on the way. Give me two minutes, and then you wake up Nims and tell her we are coming. Feed her again. And we'll have to hope it is enough." I yank the door open, next to it already for my pacing, while I talked to Duncan. I see someone passing by, and I grab their arm, "Tell Callum to get up here." The vampire hisses at me, and I give them a shake. "I'm not asking, friend. This is an emergency. Fetch him now." I give the vampire a shove toward the direction of the ball. They glare at me but head that way. I don't know if they will fetch him or not, but I don't have time to wait and see.

Striding back over to the bed, I lean over Olivia. "Wake up sleepyhead. It's time. We are going to get you home."

Her eyes open slowly, sluggish, like it is a great effort to lift her lids. "What?"

"We are going home. This very minute. Where is your laptop? I know you want to take that."

"I don't know. It was all in here when I left the room. I don't know what they did with it, or anything else I had in here for that matter."

"Fuck. All right, you stay up. If I can't find your shit, we'll go without it, and I will buy you another one." She nods. She isn't even excited about going home to Nims. Fuck me. Where would they hide her shit? Drawers. Dashing over there, I rip drawers open. Nothing. Closet? Crossing the room, I open it, jackpot. Though I don't see specifically the laptop yet, I smell her in here. I know she hasn't been in here since we brought her out of there. I rifle through the closet. When Callum walks into the room, I say, "Good! Get your plane ready. She needs to be home. Yesterday."

"We were leaving in a few hours. Isn't that soon enough?"

"No. Now. And I'm not sure that is soon enough."

"What are you doing in there?"

"Finding her stuff. Is she still up? Go be useful and feed her again."

Where the hell did they put it? I can smell her things. I spot a thin, nearly invisible line on the wall. Oh, you shady fucks. I try pressing on it, beside it, nothing happens. I can hear her protesting that she doesn't need to feed again, and Callum insisting. At least he follows directions. I don't have time to be delicate about this. Hopefully, Callum will forgive me. Balling my fist, I punch the place I suspect is the door. It crumples inward with the impact, breaking the catch as the edges fold outward.

I grab an edge and rip the door open. Her whole fucking suitcase is in here. Grabbing the handle, I try to be gentle with her things, though I just want to grab them and go already. I can hear him telling her what a good girl she is. She snarls at him. That's my girl. Suitcase freed, I give the space a cursory glance. I don't see anything else in there.

"Oh, look, they had it all packed for you. Ready to go?"

"We are really going?"

Callum's face is tight as he says, "Yes, we are taking you home to your Nims."

The words have barely left his mouth when he scoops her into his arms as he stands. He strides toward the stairs, and I follow. She isn't even fighting him about carrying her. This isn't good. I hurry around him as we get to the front door, opening it for him. A group of people are just exiting a vehicle as we get outside.

Callum says, "Oh, good, you're home. I have to leave, taking your car. The ball is going swimmingly. If anyone asks why we had to leave suddenly, it is complications from her ordeal at Diane's hands."

His father asks, "Where are you taking her?"

Callum never slows, setting her gently in the car as he says, "To the witches. They are expecting us."

Before his father can say another word, Callum is in the car, and I slide in, tucking the case off to the side as I close the door behind me. Callum raps on the window separating us from the driver. Before it finishes lowering, he says, "Airport. Get us there as fast as possible. We'll pay for any issues."

Chapter Eighteen

OLIVIA

I just want to be in my dreams with Nims. She was there with me, till we were both woke up by force. They are bustling me off somewhere, and I don't even care where it is they are taking me. What I wish is that they would let me sleep. Every time I close my eyes, they want to talk at me.

They get me tucked into an airplane, and Blair excuses himself off to the bathroom. Callum watches him go and turns to me. "I'm glad we have a moment alone. I think you have gotten some ideas about me, and how I feel about you, that aren't accurate. As you must know by now, the vampire world is a minefield. One has to take caution in letting people know who they care about." Oh, good grief, now he wants to explain how he feels. But I don't care anymore. He continues, "I think you may have overheard something I said to Diane and not known the nuance to the conversation. I care for you, deeply. But it is, and will always be, too dangerous to trust anyone with that information."

"Oh, stuff it. I don't want to hear it. Not another word! I know, I know that the vampire world is dangerous and treacherous and that everyone in it is out for number one. I hate it, and I have ever since I was dragged into it. It is all so damn ridiculous. None of you can be trusted, and all of you just want to use me for one reason or another. But lest you think I haven't been listening," I hold up a hand and tick the names off on my fingers as I list them. "Roman, Duncan, Naill, Ailsa, Blair, his mother, the tiny woman at the bookstore. Everyone I run into tells me how dangerous and untrustworthy the vampires are. I know you lot can't be trusted. That's why." I stop myself before I say things that will reveal Nims secret. "That's why I don't trust you or any other vampire. You are all out for what you can get."

"You seem awfully friendly with that damned Duncan."

"Jealousy? Do you think somewhere in that stupid pea-brain of yours that I owe any of you a relationship? Men!" I stand. Thankfully the plane is still on the ground. Heading toward the front, I find another space to sit, and I face the wall. I would just as soon not have either of them bothering me.

CALLUM

She is stunning as she storms off. I can hear her sit in a different seating space. Damn. I did not mean to let it slip about Duncan. It was not my finest moment. Especially, since I think about it, she mostly talked to him when he was connecting her and the dog. I don't get it. It really seemed like they had a relationship of some sort going on while we were there. I know she has something going with the wolf. But she had no qualms about being with me. Well, initially anyway. I'm still not certain just how I fucked this up. Perhaps it was a combination of things?

Blair walks in and, seeing her not in her seat, says, "What did you do?"

"I tried to apologize. It went poorly. It would seem talking to her is something I need to work at."

Blair laughs, "It's all that weird shit you vampires do. Always looking for a way to get one up on each other. Lies, deception, trickery. She hates all of it. And you put her square in the middle of it with your dumb shit. She was fine there with Roman's family. She had only just begun to come out of her shell, when you came along and had to take her away from everything she loves and Nims, who she can't live without."

"I told her she could bring the dog."

Blair shakes his head. "You are the least observant vampire I have ever met. I hope you don't have to walk and chew gum any time soon. I'm going to sit with her."

What is so special about that damn dog?

Duncan

All Nims wants to do is sleep. They aren't going to be here for a few hours yet, and Blair said to keep her awake. Fuck it. "Come on, Nims, we are going for a walk to pass some time till she gets here."

Nims sighs and heaves herself off the floor. I know she doesn't believe that Olivia is coming home. I don't know how to convince her. She walks with me down the stairs. I take her by the kitchen and feed her some more blood. She takes it well enough, but she stops as soon as I stop pushing her to eat. Grabbing a leash, I hook it to her collar. She doesn't need it, but it helps keep up the illusion that she is just a dog.

We head directly for the hidden magical sector. Most of

Inverness would lose their collective shit, if they realized that there is an entire magical sector right in the middle of the city that none of them have ever seen. Or will ever see. Walking through the magical wall is always a strange feeling. It is like a sentient ooze tasting me, to make sure I belong in this sector. I wonder if it feels the same to the humans?

Inside, Nims looks a little more alive. She tugs the leash toward the witch's shop. Not really my favorite place, but we'll go for her. Walking behind her, I realize how sharply her bones are standing out. Thank the gods, Olivia will be here in a few hours.

We walk in the door, and Ailsa spots Nims immediately, leaving the box she was sorting to rush over to her. Ailsa kneels before Nims, her hands cradling the fuzzy and too thin face. "Oh, baby, you miss her so bad you can hardly eat."

Nims' mouth opens and this terrible, heart-breaking howl erupts from her throat. Ailsa nods and clucks, patting her as she says, "It's ok. You go ahead and cry. We'll hear your hurts. The witches will hear you when she can't."

The sound is chilling as it goes on. The entire store is quiet, heads bowed as they listen to her. More than one person wipes away their own tears as they stand there. From down the street, answering howls ring through the air.

After an eternity and a moment, Nims falls silent and rests her head on Ailsa's shoulder. She looks up at me. "How long before Olivia arrives?"

I look at my watch. "Little under three hours. They are in the air."

When Nims lifts her head, Ailsa nods and puts her hands on either side of that fuzzy face. "She is coming back to you right now, I promise. She will be here before the sun comes up again. You just hold on a little longer, and you'll be with her."

Nims tail thumps a few times. I scoff. "What? You'll believe her, but not me? I told you the same thing not two hours ago!"

Ailsa smiles and touches a finger to the tip of Nims nose, briefly. "Of course, she believes you. But you have been saying that Olivia will come back, and you didn't listen to her. She's lonely since all the others are off with foster vampires. She lost her person and her friends. If ever she must leave them all behind again, the wolves or the witches will keep them. You do not understand dogs or companionship."

As if I needed further insult, Nims nodded in agreement. "Would you like to keep Nims here with you while I tend to some business at the bar?"

Ailsa nods. "Yes, it will do her good. We'll feed her a bit, too."

She disconnects the leash, and I drop my end of it. It disappears as Nims stands. She never looks back at me as they walk over to the space she was standing in before we arrived. Turning, I head for the bar and a stiff drink to soothe my ego while I talk to Roman.

Chapter Nineteen

Olivia

Blair comes to sit in front of me. I look at him and realize he has more food in his hands. "Where did you find food here?"

He shrugs, "It's a plane. They usually have food on planes, so I asked. Here," he holds out a forkful of something. The idea of eating kind of makes my stomach clench a little. He keeps holding the fork there, patiently watching and waiting for me to take the bite.

Rolling my eyes, I lean forward and take the food. It tastes like cardboard. I manage to force it down, but it is work. Blair looks unsure about the rest of the food after watching me choke. He sighs and pulls a small bag of blood out of his pocket. "Drink this instead. That was painful to watch. The food didn't smell like it was terrible. But no one should have to struggle with their food the way you just did."

Accepting the bag, I bite into it and start drinking. It goes down easily enough. After I finish it, I set it off to the side and watch the sky go by out the window. It's not long before

"

Blair says, "He is taking you home. You could probably forgive him a little."

"Or I could keep in mind that people always say what they really mean when they think I won't hear it. When I get home, I will be reunited with my Nims, and she will be in more danger. Do you think there is a chance in hell that he wouldn't race to tell everyone what she is the minute he found out? No, you don't, because you know I am right. He knows it, too. He was just telling me how dangerous the vampire world is, and how they cannot be trusted. Well, success. He has taught me that one thing. That vampires cannot be trusted. And I will not make that mistake again."

"You're right. The only reason Roman and company took it as well as they did is because Ailsa told them they would, or else. Duncan is all right with her, but sometimes he smells uneasy about it. Niall, I don't think you need to concern yourself about him. He was willing to stand up to Roman for you. If there is a vampire you could trust, it's him."

Smiling at the memory of Niall realizing everyone had to know what Nims is, at his realization of what she is, and how he immediately was on our side with no knowledge of the witch's edicts. I agree with Blair. "You're right. I can trust Niall. He is as new as I am and hasn't assimilated into being one of them. Yet."

Blair tilts his head as he watches me. "You grew a shell being in Italy. I'm sorry you had to, but it suits you. I think we are going to land soon. Do you want to move back in there where Callum is or stay here?"

"I will be staying here. I am not fostering any of his ideas about us. He is a mentor and maker, nothing else."

Chapter Twenty

CALLUM

She hates me. I was trying to explain, and it set her off somehow. I'm not sure how to fix this, but I will. She wants me at arm's distance, fine. I'll make her beg for my touch. Blair keeps a hand on her as they leave the plane. I follow behind them, watching her walk. She is so much more frail looking than I realized. Vampires aren't generally able to look malnourished without great effort, but she is. It hasn't been long since we freed her, but any other vampire would have devoured a small town and be hale once again. She almost seems to be pained by the idea of eating.

In the limo, she is a little more lively while watching as the scenery go by. Her hands are on her knees, and they keep opening and closing. What is so special about this dog? The driver rolls to a smooth stop at the front door of Roman's estate. Fuck, I hate being here. She is out of the car as soon as it is close to a stop. Blair follows behind, not a care in the world.

I've never seen a shifter so comfortable in a vampire estate. It's just odd. I make my way into the house to find

Olivia laying on the floor with her Nims, the two of them wrapped up in each other while Blair and Duncan watch. The damn dog notices my entrance into the house and lifts her head to look at me. She lifts a lip in a snarl and growls. Olivia whispers in her ear, and she snorts at me. The damn dog snorted at me. What the hell kind of dog is that?

Roman walks in and raises a brow at the sight of Olivia in her dress laying on the floor with Nims. He sees me, and his face closes into coldness. "Hello Callum. I see you've brought our Olivia home early. Will you be leaving, or are you continuing her training here in Scotland?"

"I will continue her training here. The air in Italy was too dry for Olivia, and it made for a less than healthy environment."

Roman nods. "You are welcome to stay in the house if you like. Olivia and Nims have their own permanent set of rooms."

"I would like to discuss some things with you, Roman. Is there somewhere private we can speak, while they get reacquainted?"

Roman's eyes glint with speculation, though his face is a rock. "Yes. My enforcer, Niall, will be with us, or does it need to be more private than that?"

"It pains me to say it, but I know Duncan. If you wish to have an enforcer with you, let it be him."

He nods, "Very well. Duncan, you're with me. Niall, you stay with Olivia and Nims. See if you can't get the two of them to eat something."

Niall steps out from behind Roman. "We'll get them fed. I've got the kitchen working on some things Olivia might have missed while she was away."

Roman gestures for me to follow him. Duncan falls in

beside me. We all walk in silence as Roman leads us to one of his offices further away from where everyone else is.

The office he leads us to is small and fairly sparse. Nothing like the main one he usually sees people in. Seating himself behind the desk, he says, "This room is even more heavily soundproofed than my other office. It seemed like you might need to speak secrets."

"Yes. I do. Did you realize that my father was on the panel for Olivia's hearing?"

"I suspected it was a relative."

Seating myself in one of the chairs, I think about it again before I say more. My father will consider this treason to the family, if he ever finds out about this conversation. But Olivia's safety must come first. "While we were at the family estate for the vampire ball in our area, Diane imprisoned Olivia with the intent of starving her to death." Duncan's hands curl into fists, while Roman tents his fingers in front of his face. "Diane is, or was at the time of our leaving, imprisoned in her room. I do not expect much more than that to happen. In fact, I think it is likely that this will be quietly swept under the rug, if my father can't use it to his advantage somehow. What I'm saying is Olivia has to become part of your family for her safety. Diane will not forget the stain on her supposed honor that is Olivia. No matter that Olivia is innocent and a victim. The only way to erase the dishonor is to erase Olivia, if she is part of our family. If she is your family, well, it transfers Diane's ire, but that won't matter. Her ire is very little to worry about without the backing of the family."

Roman stares into the distance for some time after I finish speaking. When he does speak, I am floored. "What happens to you after you help us to adopt Olivia?"

My tongue slips up to press on my canine tooth, it's sharp

point providing the little pain that regulates my thinking, helps me to stay sharp and clear. "It is very probable that I will be commanded home and punished."

"I see. Will the punishment leave the Mezzasalma family minus another member?"

"It will. What I am doing is no less than treason in my father's eyes. As long as Olivia is safe, I can be sacrificed."

Duncan nods in approval. I don't like that we agree, but on this we do. I know he would do the same for her, lining up actions to ensure her safety, even if it would cost his life. Roman seems to be thinking hard about this. I can almost see his mind moving pieces about in his head. Then, he says, "I think we can win without your direct assistance. I would rather keep an ally in secret than to have them sacrificed for poor planning. Tell me everything about why you were not able to fulfill your role as mentor to her. What family attacked you? Perhaps, I can search out some old secrets that will help."

Chapter Twenty-One

My Nims crashes into me at the entry. We both fall to the floor as I wrap my arms around her. Neither of us moves beyond snuggling into each other. Having her fuzzy face against mine again is such a relief. I don't even know how long we lay there, soaking up the presence of each other. I hear voices, but they don't matter. Then, a hand touches my shoulder, and Niall says, "Hey, I know you two are enjoying being reunited, but maybe you could both come eat? You know, so I don't get in trouble with the boss. Help a guy out?"

I can't hold back my laugh at the way he is cajoling us into eating. I have no doubt it is true to some extent. But I am entertained anyway. I give Nims one more squeeze and tell her, "I don't know about you, but I find myself famished."

Nims does a quiet bark of agreement, and we both get up from the floor. Niall asks, "Can I have a hug? We are all glad you are home again."

I open my arms to welcome him over for a hug. Nims

wedges herself between us, making sure she is part of the hug. He whispers in my ear, "You look like hell, and so does your dog. Come eat, the both of you." He releases us, and I catch a glimpse of us in the mirror. I see what he means. We look fucking rough. We are both underweight, and the effects of that reflect in my hair and skin, and in Nims fur. "Come on, let's go fatten us up a little."

Blair falls in step with us as we follow Niall. He leads us to a smallish dining room. The table nearly groans with the amount of food he has on it. My stomach growls, and so does Nims. I walk over and pull out a chair for her. She hops in, turns, and settles herself in a seated position. I slide the chair forward, so she can reach easily. Niall starts filling a plate. "I'll keep Nims fed. You work on feeding you."

Blair seats himself to the left of me as I fill my plate. I think he understands that I have to stay next to Nims, that I have missed her presence in my life more than any person. As I sit between Nims and Blair, my plate is piled high with food. Niall sits to the right of Nims after setting her plate before her. She looks at me, waiting to see me start eating before she will. The hollows in her face are prominent, and I hate it. Grabbing my fork, I dig in to the food. As I eat, I watch to make sure she is eating. Thankfully, she is.

We eat in silence for a while. Niall has been watching us eat and says, "So, what happened that Callum needs to speak with Roman in private?"

Blair snorts, "His mother tried to kill Olivia. That's why I had to go to Italy."

Nims growls briefly and continues eating.

Blair nods, "I agree. She should die for her bullshit. She hasn't yet, and I don't think it very likely that his father will do anything more about it. He didn't exactly rush home, and from what I saw, she had been ruling things in the area."

Niall stands to refill Nims' plate as she watches eagerly. He pours a bowl of blood for her and sets that next to her plate. As he seats himself again, he says, "That is because he was tricked into marrying her. He was supposed to be marrying the eldest daughter of her clan. From what I have seen in my research, it was an enormous scandal at the time. They had him believing he was marrying the eldest right up till the vows had been said and the ink dried. This part is only rumor, but it is said that he had it bad for the eldest he wanted, and he wasn't marrying into their family for power or money because they didn't have either. When he found out he had been tricked, that they had fooled him and her, he swore vengeance on the other family. Only, he couldn't really do shit because he was bound by the marriage contract. Vampires value the keeping of contracts over just about anything."

"Didn't Callum say something about a contract being broken?"

Blair grins, "He did."

Niall looks away. "I certainly would not want to be the woman who had taken part in that scandal and had later broken the contract that kept me safe. She may not die for what she did to Olivia, but I don't think that she is going to be a problem for you ever again."

CALLUM

We are still discussing Olivia's safety when my phone rings. Pulling it out of my pocket, I see my father is calling. "I have to take this. Please, remain silent, so he thinks I am alone." They both nod their agreement, and I answer. "Hello, Father."

"We have a problem. Diane was not working alone."

My eyes meet Roman's. "What do you mean, she wasn't working alone?"

"We were still discussing the transfer of power when someone entered her room through a secret door. A man from a large, religious organization. He was quite surprised to see us with Diane. After everything calmed down again, we questioned them. Olivia was due to be picked up by these people the day you set her free. They wanted her weakened because they are all human. Son, they want her bad. Is she aware that they are after her? Were you?"

Roman inclines his head a millimeter to indicate I should share this with my father. What a strange world I have stepped into. "Yes. We had hoped that her time in Italy would throw them off her trail. I don't think anyone could have guessed that one of our own would be working with them."

Father snarls, "She is not one of us. Her life is forfeit for this second betrayal to the family. I will let you know any further information I receive from her as regards Olivia. Watch your back. I have yet to ferret out who all is loyal to her."

"I will. Be safe, Father."

"And you."

The call ends and I shove the phone back in my pocket. Roman's face is stone. Duncan's face is a little more expressive in that he looks furious, if silent and in control. Roman is the one I am concerned with, as he wields the power in this situation. He breaks his silence, saying, "We are putting the family on high alert. I'm still not sure why they want her so bad. If your father finds out, please share that information. In light of that call, do you want to put the idea of helping us to adopt Olivia on hold?"

He's giving me a way out? What the hell kind of vampire is so honorable when they could press their advantage? I breathed and responded, "No, but perhaps we could do a shared adoption. She remains part of our family, but as you all were part of her life before I could be, perhaps it would be fair that she be part of your family, too."

A slight raising of a brow is all the reaction Roman displays beyond his nod. "I would agree with those terms. Will your father and the rest of the council?"

"Possibly, if we present it to them the right way."

BLAIR

Olivia finally looks like herself. So does Nims. The two of them devoured food and blood until, finally, they both leaned back with a sigh. Niall led us to a sitting room where Olivia and Nims curled themselves into a large chair to talk to each other. Niall looks at me and says, "I almost feel like I am intruding. Want a drink?"

"Yes, please." I seat myself in the chair to the left of Olivia's. Close but also near the couch, so I can chat with Niall while we wait. He hands me a drink and sits on the couch near me, just as Callum and Duncan walk in with another heated conversation going between the two of them. Niall looks at me and raises a brow before turning to watch them.

"I brought her back so she could live in her home, not so you could cloister her up in this monstrosity you call a house."

"It is not a monstrosity, and she stays here. Doing that keeps her safe."

"The baroque era would like their flourishes back. You're right, it isn't a monstrosity, it is a crime against taste. She will have me with her. And Blair, who hasn't left her side since he appeared on my doorstep one day."

That almost sounded like an insult. Reaching over, I tap Olivia on the shoulder. She and Nims both look at me. "I don't know if you noticed, but they are discussing you."

The temperature of the room goes up a couple degrees, and silence falls between Duncan and Callum. Olivia asks, "What, exactly, is it about me that you two are discussing, as if I am not sitting right here?"

Callum folds his arms across his chest. "Let's tell her, shall we, Duncan?"

Duncan scowls, and the temperature of the room goes up even further. I focus on Olivia. Though she seems calm, the room heating with her displeasure is new. Duncan says, "Again, I am thinking of your safety. You should stay here, where there are many more vampires to take care of you, should the time call for it."

She raises a palm out toward him, and he falls silent. "I will be staying in my house. I am fine with whatever security protocols Roman thinks are appropriate, but I will be in my home again. Fuck, I have had more than enough of people telling me where I will stay. Where are the rest of my dogs?"

Duncan runs a hand across the back of his neck. "Well, um, you see."

"I do not see a single one of them, and I have asked you where they are." The temperature of the room goes up a little more. What the hell is happening here?

Duncan swallows and says, "They were kind of adopted out. Which is good right? You wanted them all to have good homes. Even the ones you thought would live with you forever because they couldn't trust humans. They got homes.

The vampires here, they all love dogs, and the dogs kind of chose them." The temperature in the room returns to normal, and I am more than a little glad Duncan got to explaining fast. "Even the one that was blind in one eye and had that permanent limp?"

"Twitchy?"

"Yes! Twitchy! Twitchy went with Elspeth, who took one look at him and fell in love. She said he reminded her of the dog she had when she was human. He was the first to go. She didn't meet with Roman, like she had planned. She took the dog down to the shifter's shop and bought everything he could possibly want. Incidentally, Blair's mom asks that you hold off on adopting out any more dogs. They are waiting on a shipment of dog supplies."

The room temperature is fully back to normal as Olivia says, "That's wonderful. I'll need to meet them all, just for my peace of mind. You can send them by my house. We are ready to go home now. Would you prefer we go in a car, or shall we have an exciting walk?"

Duncan groans as he presses the heels of his palms into his eyes and then shoves his hands through his hair, leaving it a mess. "Fine. If you don't mind, please wait a moment while I arrange for the car and check in with Roman as to what safety protocol he would have in place."

She smiles brightly at him, "Of course. Don't be too long, I might forget the car and start walking."

Niall claps his hand over his mouth as Duncan spins on his heel and leaves the room. Callum laughs openly. Then, he sobers and asks Olivia, "Would you introduce me to your Nims?"

Nims growls at him, and Olivia says, "I don't think she is ready to accept you. She tends to hold a grudge. It's better that way. You are here to be my mentor and nothing else. You don't need to be close to my girl. She isn't your business. We will finish this mentoring arrangement because I have learned things from you, and I see the value in that. Once it is done, once the year is finished, you can take yourself back to Italy, where you belong."

Chapter Twenty-Two

OLIVIA

This is not my house. I know my house, and this is not it. I guess it must have burnt fully to the ground. Even the fence is different. Nims and I are standing on the sidewalk, staring up at it. Blair stands on one side, while Callum stands on the other. Duncan has grabbed my suitcase from the back and walks over. "They did a pretty good job rebuilding it. It isn't quite the same, but we didn't have any pictures of how it looked before. Come, let's see if you like the changes that Roman made."

I notice the door has a digital lock. That's kind of nice. I see it has a keypad, but also a fingerprint scanner. Duncan uses it and lets us in, saying, "We'll get that wiped and your print installed tomorrow, or tonight, when you prefer." He sets my bag off to the side. "Roman took some liberties with the space available, and he made the house wider to accommodate some ideas he had. You have escape routes from your office and your bedroom, as well as the basement. Technically, they all connect, so you could send the dogs into the basement, lead them up to your bedroom, and then go back to meet the dogs in the basement. But, uh, hopefully you don't have to do that, right?"

Callum rolls his eyes, "If she has to do that, none of us are worth a damn." Blair laughs, and Duncan shrugs. "When I talked to Roman, he told me that all the security protocols he wanted implemented had already been installed. There are cameras that feed into his security room. He has a team that works around the clock monitoring his home and, now, yours. He kept the cameras out of what he thought would be your personal spaces. Like your office. The bathroom. We hadn't really paid much attention to everything in your house, so we were guessing about aesthetics. If you hate it, we can get something different. We couldn't replace the pictures. If you have digital versions, we could get them reprinted. Since he was changing the shape of your house anyway, he added a couple of extra bedrooms. They aren't huge, but they helped to account for the extra space used by the passages. But you should go ahead and explore it for yourself. Maybe start with your office?"

He crosses the hall and opens the door to the room he is calling my office. Nims stays at my side as I walk in. It is bare, no life to it, but it has the basis for a good office. Giant desk like I prefer, though the style is modern. All clean lines and boredom. They lined the walls with shelves, so that is good. Crossing the room, I stop next to the window. They put in a seat. It's shaped like a shallow crescent moon, points turned up toward the sky. It needs more pillows, but it looks cozy. Maybe a set of dark, gauzy curtains to frame it.

A mostly blank canvas.

I'm not unhappy about what I've seen so far. Turning, I walk through the rest of the downstairs. Like the office, it is fairly normal and kind of boring. The kitchen is a bright, sunny yellow. It has a lot of the little touches that made it a gorgeous, older house. Before. The back door has a window, like the one before had. I look through it, and the backyard looks oddly bigger. The basement is large and empty of all my stores. Guess I'll have to restock over time.

The men have been following in silence as Nims and I explore the house. We head upstairs, and I immediately see that there are more doors than should be up here. Two doors on the left are bedrooms, another to the right. The last door in the hall is before me, and I open it slowly, remembering the last time I was in here. It looks nothing like I remember, though I can see it is meant to be the primary bedroom. It is larger than the others. There are two doors to one side of the room. One is a bathroom. It is nice and fairly spacious. The other is a closet. I see an odd seam on the back wall. Nims is over sniffing it right after I notice it. Getting closer, I press on one side of the seam and it pops open. Ah, the passage. It should be well hidden, once I put some clothing in here.

Pressing the door closed, I exit the closet. Everyone is gathered in the doorway. Duncan asks, "Is it? Does it work for you?"

"Yes, it's fine. I need to add some things, but it's fine. For now, I just want some space. I understand you all are going to be here, but you can't be so clingy. Go do something. If I can't be safe alone in my house, then there is nowhere I will be safe."

Blair chuckles, "That's our cue. Out, gentlemen, don't make me bite you."

Callum's tongue presses against a canine tooth. "Better be careful, I might like it, wolfman."

Well, this ranks pretty high on the shit I don't need scale. "I said out. If you all can't act like adults, you can't be here."

Nims adds her own growl to back me up. They all turn

and leave the room. Blair gives me a strange look before he goes. I hear grumbles, but nothing distinct. Nims follows behind them, shoving the door shut once they clear the threshold.

Duncan

She stays holed up in that bedroom with Nims for hours. We all separate and find our own spaces to occupy in the house. I choose the porch out back. She is probably going to be pissed when she figures out that Roman bought the places surrounding hers and had the houses moved to other properties, allowing her to have a much larger yard and more space between her house and the neighbors' yards.

He said I should avoid mentioning it for as long as possible. I don't know if I agree. She seemed to notice something was different about the backyard already. Luckily, the witches are fully in support of anything that might keep Olivia safe, and they helped. If they hadn't, this far end of the yard would still show the bare space where they took out the old house.

I'm still lost in thought when she walks out onto the porch. Nims is with her and comes over to give me a nudge, so I'll pet her. I may not be her person, but she doesn't hate me anymore, and she might even like me a little bit now.

Olivia sits next to me in one of the chairs and says, "Who chose these?"

"Roman. He said this porch reminded him of a place he was happy. So he chose chairs that felt like that place."

"It must have been a good place. What did he do with my neighbors?

"Er, what do you mean?"

"Did you all really think I wouldn't notice that my closest neighbors are not here any more?"

"We might have hoped that it would take a little longer."

She laughs and shakes her head. "You all have been insulated in your little vampire world for entirely too long. Willing to pretend you don't notice an entire building or three disappearing to avoid possibly offending someone and go do sneaky research later. You could be direct and ask the question. If they are so weird as to get upset about that, they need to check themselves."

Chuckling, I tell her, "I get your point, but this is vampire society. It is the way things are. As a society, we are pretty set in our ways. Changing our society as a whole is well beyond what I am capable of doing."

"Maybe it does need to change. Maybe it just needs the right person to push for the changes."

The thought of her taking on changing the vampire world is a little terrifying. She barely has an understanding of it. "Maybe, maybe you could. I think you should first get to know it and fully understand it. I know you already feel like you know more than enough about it, and what you do know, you don't like. You should never take on an enemy without knowing them inside and out. You need to know how they would come at you. Then, you can thwart them at every turn."

She smiles at me and leans closer. "You know, you're kind of sexy when you are helping me figure out how to overthrow vampire society."

Her scent surrounds me as she leans in. Every fiber of my being wants to crush her to me. She has no idea the siren call she is simply by existing. Every ounce of control I have concentrates on holding myself in place. Her lips touch mine, and my iron will smashes into a thousand pieces. My arms go round her, grabbing her and dragging her into my lap.

Her light kiss becomes fierce and demanding, her hands on my shoulders as she maneuvers herself to straddle my legs. My hands slip under her shirt to feel her skin, hot to the touch. She moans into my mouth when my hands cup her breasts. Breaking the kiss, I push her back, so I can snatch her shirt up and off her body. The bra cups take only an instant to slip under her breasts, and then I have one of her big nipples in my mouth, sucking hard on it as she tangles her fingers in my hair. Her moans as I move to the other nipple have me thinking about getting those pants off her. Then, she freezes as someone clears their throat. She pushes my head away from her breast, and I turn to look at the rude asshole. "What the fuck do you want that can't wait?"

Callum is standing there, his face a mask, other than his tongue worrying at his canine tooth. "It is time for Olivia's lessons. While I'm certain you don't care if she knows about the vampire world, I do. We are not missing them, so you can get your dick wet. Do that on your own time."

Olivia slides off my lap, those beautiful breasts tucked back in her bra. She grabs her shirt and pulls it back on. Standing, I adjust myself and grab Olivia by the waist, crushing her to me. Grabbing her hair with my other hand, I pull her head back and to the side, exposing her neck to me. Licking up the side of her throat, I get to her ear and whisper, "We'll finish this later, when the wet blanket is done with your lessons for the day."

She is breathing heavy still when I release her. She tries to speak and has to stop to clear her throat, "Um, Nims, let's go do my lessons for the night."

Callum, watching all this time, spins on his heel and

stands in the kitchen, holding the door open for her. She puts a hand on my chest, gives it a pat, and heads into the house. I watch, and when Callum closes the door as he looks at me with daggers in his eyes, I simply adjust my erection with a smile.

Chapter Twenty-Three

CALLUM

That dog pays attention to every word we say. And she looks like that dog Olivia wouldn't leave that night. But Nims can't be that dog. It's been at least a decade, and this dog is young. Once Olivia is in the house, and I've shut the door on Duncan, I ask her, "Where would you prefer to have our lessons tonight?"

"In the living area. I think there is furniture enough for us to sit in there."

I motion for her to lead the way, and she does. Her hips are fucking distracting. I hate that Duncan was between her thighs, and I can't be. She smells delicious when she is turned on like this. Fuck! Focus, Callum. She thinks you hate her or something. You cannot simply bury your face between those thighs. No matter how much you want to, she doesn't want you. Or at least, she has decided not to want me. I can smell it when she is turned on by me. But she isn't consenting , dammit.

She seats herself on the couch, and the dog sits on the floor next to her. Seating myself on the same couch, I turn to face her, folding one leg up onto the cushion. "Would you prefer to feed now or at the end of the lesson?"

She shrugs, "May as well get it over with."

I clamp down hard on my emotions. She doesn't need to deal with any of this. Unbuttoning the cuff of my sleeve, I roll it up and extend my naked wrist to her. She leans forward, takes my wrist in her hands, and sinks her fangs into it, all while keeping her eyes focused on mine. The exquisite pain has me inhaling at the release I feel with it, my eyelids dropping to close briefly. When I open them again, she is still watching me as she feeds. I can't help but picture her with her mouth around my cock and those beautiful eyes looking up at me. Jesus, focus Callum! Keep that shit tamped down until she requests it.

She finishes feeding and releases my arm, wiping at the corners of her mouth. She didn't spill a drop, but she does that every time. I could watch her do that every day until forever ends.

She retreats back into herself. Nothing of her personality is available because I am not to be trusted, and I don't know how to earn it back. "What would you like to learn?"

She immediately says, "Vampire society."

"That was fast. Why the sudden interest?"

"Someone pointed out that I should know it inside and out, if I want to make changes to it. I would like to know everything about vampire society, and why it is the way it is. Why do they cling so hard to traditions, and the insistence that this is the way it has always been done? Why are they so against change?"

"Ah, I see. I suppose, to start with, you need to know how we became. Unlike other creatures, our origins are fairly well-documented. It started as you would imagine, with a man wanting more power and not reading the fine print.

Demons have always existed, and they seem to enjoy messing with humans. There are different varieties of demons. Many varieties. The one we are focused on, it was fairly high ranking in their society and powerful. So, when this man seeking power found the demon's name and called it forth, the demon was not pleased. It was curious, though. They let the man tell him of their demands for power in the mortal world."

"Wait, they called a powerful, high-ranking demon just to gain power in the human world? Really?"

"Yes. Really. He said he wanted to be at the top of the food chain. It is said that the demon laughed and asked the man if he was sure that is what he wants. The man insisted that was exactly what he wanted, to be the most powerful man on earth. The demon clapped his hands, and power flashed white. Suddenly, the man was taken by a terrible lust for blood. He wanted to berate the demon and make him change things, but the demon was gone. No matter how the man did the ritual after that, he could not call the demon back."

"How did he know it was blood he craved?"

"The demon told him, his voice ringing out even after he was gone. He told him that his wish was granted and that he would live forever, becoming more powerful every year, but chained to his need for blood. Worse yet, he had no control over his thirst in those first years. He laid waste to entire tribes, and when he figured out that he could make others like himself, he created an army. He swept the continent like a plague."

"How did humans survive?" she asked, rapt in her interest.

"Because humans are many and cunning, and once the survival instinct kicks in, they band together to become nearly unstoppable. They figured out how to kill his followers. His followers began to disappear into the night, when they realized they were being hunted. Finally, there was only him left. The humans quickly found that they could not kill him. So they cut him into pieces and they hid those pieces in secret places. Keeping him from regenerating because the rest of him was still out there, intact. Those tribes, the guardians of his pieces, are the reason why we have vampire hunters today. They know we exist and just how much destruction we can cause, if we are not kept in check. The few vampires that escaped the original hunt, they found each other and created the council, along with the rules that vampires were to live by in order to escape detection by the guardian tribes. Most of us have forgotten about the tribes. It is only a very few families that keep the memory and push for our society to remain true to the original rules that kept us safe."

"How did we get from these rules to keep the guardian tribes from killing us to, here is this entire society based around everyone behaving in certain ways or they are terrible and should be killed for their transgressions?"

"The simple answer is power. Most humans lust for it, and that doesn't change when they become vampires. So, they patterned our society after that of the humans. The rise to power in our society happens only in these ways that are carefully controlled, and who can access those ways is even more carefully regulated and monitored."

The entire time we are talking, Nims watches us. None of the usual dog behaviors of favoring distraction. Like most working dogs, this dog is clocking me. I can see her focus on everything we are talking about. It is the weirdest behavior I have ever seen in a dog. Then Olivia says, "You really have so much knowledge locked away. It's a shame that you are so fully entrenched in the way vampire society is. That you are too scared to buck the system."

"I have never had a reason to buck the system. No reason to fight it."

"And perhaps you wouldn't recognize a reason, if it bit you daily." She snorts, "I'm sorry that things didn't work out between us. I need a loyalty that you don't understand. And I won't be going back to Italy with you, either. I don't care what anyone says, and the courts can shove it up their collective asses."

"I wouldn't ask you to go back there. I can see you need to be with your dog. Though, I wish you would talk to me about her. Tell me why she couldn't go with you."

Her face closes like she had never confided in me. "You can't be trusted with me. I sure as hell will not be trusting you with her. We are done for the night. Have a pleasant day."

I watch her stand and leave the room, the dog right at her side the entire time. I've never seen a dog get just as frosty as its owner the way this one did.

I need to know what Olivia is hiding.

DUNCAN

Niall is telling me about recent developments within the family when Callum walks in. Niall falls silent as soon as he hears the footsteps, because not everyone should know about the good or bad things happening within our family. We wait as Callum walks in and stops at one of the empty seats at the kitchen table. Facing us, his tongue slips up to worry at his canine tooth. He is silent a moment longer before he says, "Duncan, I need to speak to you. Alone, preferably."

Looking closer at him, I know he is wound tight over

Olivia. I would laugh, but I find myself feeling a little sympathy for him, even if he is a cockblocker. "If you are looking for insight into Olivia, and I feel certain you are, you are going to want Niall here to stay. He is, I think, her best friend after Nims."

Callum looks angry and jealous. Niall laughs. "You have it as bad for her as Duncan and Blair. Well, I'll be nicer to you than I was to Duncan. I am the one person in this house that you don't have to worry is fucking Olivia. I obviously need to be a bit more flamboyant, as neither of you noticed I am as gay as the day is long in the summer. So, you may as well sit and relax. Quit scowling like it would make a difference if I wasn't gay. She is gorgeous and kind and funny and smarter than any of you give her credit for being. If I was even slightly inclined her way, I would take her from all of you. Except maybe Blair. He seems to have a fair handle on things."

Callum relaxes visibly. Seating himself, he says, "Tell me about the dog."

Fuck. Niall tenses and we share a look. Taking a breath, I ask him, "Why do you want to know about her?"

Callum looks down at the table. "I can't protect Olivia from our family, if I don't know what I am protecting. I know there is something about that dog. I haven't quite put my finger on it. I feel certain that, if my father sees that dog, he is going to sense the something off and kill it on sight. I need to know what I am protecting."

Niall and I look at each other, unsure what we should, what we can say. Then, Olivia speaks from behind me, "In protecting Nims, you are protecting my heart and soul. Nothing more and nothing less. She is all the best parts of me and without her, I won't survive."

Chapter Twenty-Four

OLIVIA

The silence is thick in the room after what I said. Niall looks at me with such compassion. He knows how much Nims means to me. He realized it before the rest of them. Callum, he is concerned. His shock prevents him from maintaining his usual mask of aloofness. He looks a little frightened even. If I had to guess, I would say that is because of my catching him trying to ask about my Nims.

I don't think I have any choice but to tell him. He has already noticed that she is different. It is only a matter of time till he puts it together, the same as Duncan and Niall did. At least, if Callum finds out now and can't deal with it, I have people to help me.

Walking into the kitchen, I take one of the other seats at the table. "Nims is part of the family. You turned her at the same time as you turned me. I was laying so close to her," I put a hand on her for comfort. The memories still hurt. "I was laying so close to her that, when the blood splashed, it went in her mouth, too. She is the reason I survived. If not for her, I would have died or exposed us by accident. She is the reason

I made it this far, and I am her reason. When I woke up that next evening, I didn't understand how we were alive. How she was alive. I carried her home in my arms, sure that she would die, and I would follow her. Instead, as morning came, I passed out after being unable to find a vet that would take payments. She taught me everything. Made our first kill. She knew I needed to drink blood when I was completely ignorant of the possibility that vampires were real. That I was one."

Callum swallows, "She is the dog you wouldn't leave that night. How many people know what she is?"

Niall answers while Duncan watches Callum closely. "Most of the Slora family. All the witches and the shifters. The witches have decreed that if she dies, if they die, we all do. I don't think they will have any issues with wiping out two vampire families."

Callum's jaw drops and snaps back up as he says, "What?"

Duncan nods. "The witches have quite firmly stated that these two are important and must be protected at all costs. From within our ranks and without. Has Olivia mentioned the religious nutjobs?" Duncan raises his brows oddly. If I had to guess, they spoke about the church being after me.

Callum says, "I am aware of them, but I don't know the full story."

At Callum's no, he explains about them and why her house isn't exactly like it was. He tells him that there are cameras throughout the house. Callum isn't surprised about the cameras. I guess he probably noticed them. They aren't really hidden. He asks, "Did the witches say why? Why it is that the two of them are so important?"

Duncan snarls, "No. It's a constant source of irritation for us all."

"The question now is, what will you do with this

information?" All eyes are on me as soon as I ask, but Duncan's go right back to watching Callum.

Callum says, "Keep you far away from my father and the rest of the family. You have to be adopted into Roman's family. My father prefers to have us in our home region. If you are part of the family, he will insist on it. He is going to fight about the adoption. And I am going to fight for you to be a part of the Slora family. My father is vicious and uncompromising. If he thinks you are valuable, he will do everything in his power to claim you and make sure that everything you do benefits our family. When he sees Nims, he'll kill her on sight. You were right to keep her here, and bringing you back to be with her is the only smart thing I have done since I saw your picture on the back cover of your book."

BLAIR

I hate leaving Olivia alone with them. I know she is safe, but I worry they aren't smart enough to recognize the signs of an imminent combustion. And I am afraid that is exactly what is going to happen to Olivia if she gets upset.

The rooms heating around her. I have a feeling it means something big is coming. But I don't know enough about magical things, and I don't want to worry her if it is nothing. The witches will know, I hope.

The shop is open by the time I arrive. They usually close it long enough to let their cleaning spells work undisturbed, but it does mean there are certain hours that I could not show up with questions. The witch behind the counter is no nonsense when I ask to speak to Ailsa. "What do you need Ailsa for? She is quite busy."

"I — this might sound silly, but a friend of mine." I didn't think this would be so difficult to explain. "My friend, rooms have been heating up around her when she gets upset. I am worried."

The witch's eyes go round, and she says, "Wait here, please."

She rushes off through the doors to the back room. Less than a minute passes, and she is back at the door, motioning for me to follow her. She guides me to Ailsa's office. This time, it looks like a kitchen. That and her long robe make me think I have disturbed her before she would ordinarily be at the shop. "I'm sorry for seeking you so early. This is the first chance I have had to get away since we got back."

She chuckles, "Sit." A chair slides out from the table a bit, and I walk over to seat myself because I am surely not going to argue with her. "If I didn't believe what you had to say was important, I wouldn't have let Ravian bring you back here. Tell me about Olivia and your concerns. I will make you tea."

I'm not overly thrilled about the tea as I prefer coffee, but again, I'm not arguing with her about it. Taking a breath, I tell her about the room heating up when Olivia was upset. How she seemed not to notice or realize it was happening. Ailsa sets a cup of something that smells similar to coffee before me and seats herself in the chair next to me with her own cup that smells floral.

I take a sip of my cup, and I am pleasantly surprised at the taste. She smiles and says, "It's chicory and dandelion. Very similar to coffee, but better for you and more sustainable. As for what is happening with Olivia, has anyone else noticed?"

"No, she is surrounded by vampires most of the time. Coincidentally, they are the ones irritating her to the point of heating the room."

She laughs, "Vampires do get full of themselves,

especially the men. They are much more prone to it. Roman is a good example of a vampire completely full of himself."

That's odd. He always seemed fairly open to things. He is always good to the shifters and everyone else. I wonder. No, I don't have time to wonder. "Is it important that no one knows? And what about Olivia? Shouldn't she know?"

"No. I would like to tell her, but all signs point to her trying to contain it if she knows. I don't know that Inverness could survive that kind of explosion. It is better for everyone if she is kept in the dark. She'll understand why I insisted on that once I tell her such is the safer option for all involved. And it's the only path I see where Nims lives. None of us fare well if Nims dies. After she explodes, bring her here. No one can know this is coming, except for the three of you that are going to be always around her."

"Can we trust Callum? Olivia doesn't, and Nims doesn't like him."

"I know. But he is deeper than he appears and more devoted to her than any of you suspect. Maybe he isn't going to suddenly be pro-Slora family, but he will forever be hers. Much like you. And Duncan. The three of you could no more leave her than you could stop being yourselves. For all that she will love you all as well, it's Nims that is her soul. Without Nims, we'll all lose. Not just her, we'll lose so much more. Keep them safe. We are watching. I'll leave word at the counter that you are to be brought back any time you ask to speak to me. Don't abuse the privilege. Go, you have things to do today beyond talking with old witches about important people."

My mind is spinning with what she said. "I have one more question, if you don't mind? Will she be okay after she explodes? Will she hurt Nims by accident?"

"Yes. One of you will need to get Nims out of the line of fire."

Fuck. Leaving the shop, I message Duncan.

Where are you

At Olivia's. Where else would I be?

I need to talk to you. And Callum. But not in front of Olivia. Can Niall come stay with her for a little bit?

Sure. He is here now. Where do you want to meet?

The Common bar in the sector.

We'll be there in five.

Five minutes seems like an eternity as I wait for them. They walk in and spot me in my corner immediately. The two of them are such opposites. Callum is the one that asks upon sitting down, "Why do we all need to talk without Olivia?"

"Because it's about her, and she can't know yet. That isn't my choice, but it's what the witches say, and I trust them."

Callum asks, "Ailsa?" When I nod he starts messing with that canine tooth again, his tongue quickly starts bleeding. "What did Ailsa tell you?"

"It started with what I told her." I relay the entire conversation to them, minus the parts about them and myself.

Callum listens intently and nods when I finish. "I noticed the temperature change, but I didn't put it together that she was the cause. How did you?"

"Because it only happened when you all were pissing her off."

Duncan chuckles, "Well, I suppose that is a bit like a neon

sign. So, we have to watch for her getting close to an explosion, and make sure Nims is safe when it happens?"

I nod. "Essentially. Ailsa made it clear that everything goes bad for everyone, if something happens to Nims, and especially if Olivia thinks it was her fault."

Callum nods, his face grim. "Gentlemen, we know what we have to do. I am going back to Olivia. I feel it is safe to assume that we will be coordinating to ensure that the two of them have at least one of us with them at all times. To that end, here is my number." He pulls a case out of his pocket and slides two cards out, handing them to us. "Message as you please. I will do whatever is needed to help her. She is my focus for the foreseeable future."

He leaves after we accept the cards. Duncan shakes his head, staring off in the direction Callum went. "He's got it bad, and she doesn't trust him. He knows about Nims at least."

"Oh?"

"Yes. He said she has to be adopted into the Slora family. For her safety."

"No shit? What is his father going to say about that?"

"Nothing good. I need to go tend to some things with Roman. I'll be back at Olivia's in a few hours."

"I'll see you there. I am going to put in a couple of hours at the store and then head back myself."

Chapter Twenty-Five

Olivia

The writing went well today. I have been in here for hours, long enough that Nims came over to nudge me about food for the second time. "Ok, we'll go find dinner. I'm sorry. I just needed to finish that section before I lost the thread."

Nims chuffs at me.

"I know, I know. Look, I'm closing the computer now."

I stand and stretch, because even vampires get a little stiff after sitting so long in one spot. As I open the door to head for the kitchen, I see Callum reading in a chair that he has moved to the hall. "What, what are you doing here?"

"Waiting. Are you done for the day?"

"I am. Or at least for long enough to get some food. Why?"

"Let me take you both out to have dinner. We can go to the magical sector. We won't have to worry about your religious stalkers there, and we can talk vampire history."

"Covered all your bases here. All right. I need food, and the magic sector is happy to serve Nims. Let me put on some outside clothing, and we can go."

He nods and sits to wait as Nims and I head upstairs. We are back within a few minutes, and I collect the leash hanging on a hook near the door. Snapping it to her collar, we follow Callum out the door, closing it behind us. We are fairly quiet and on guard as we walk through the space between home and the magic sector. The place he takes us to is crowded and smells like heaven. I order a chicken masala, and Nims gets a couple skewers of meat. Callum orders naan for both of us and gets a curry.

The food is amazing, and our conversation is fire. He tells me about great and terrible things that vampires have done in the creation of our society. He also tells us about the jerk that turned all his hunting dogs and caused the law about dogs. Callum knew him and had told him that if he was going to turn dogs, he needed to choose ones that liked him because his hunting dogs despised him.

I file that away for later use when I start working to change the law. Hiding Nims will not work forever. We leave the restaurant, and Callum asks, "Would you care to walk around? Explore the area?"

"Will you tell me more? I love learning history in general, but vampire history is even more fascinating."

He smiles, "If that is what you wish, yes."

We walk, stopping to look at various shops as he teaches me about how the council started wars in order to distract from vampires that had gone rogue while they hunted them down. "So how often do vampires—"

Hands grab me and snatch me into an alley. Nims is on them immediately. Striking out with my elbows, I connect with a rib cage, and Nims is trying to rip off one of his legs as I spin around. I see Callum fighting a couple of guys as I punch this one in his fucking face. Unfortunately, he doesn't go down, and he lands his own blow, knocking me into the wall.

That's when he grabs Nims and throws her. I watch in horror as she hits a wall and slides down it to lie motionless. The pain of the thought that she might be gone races through my body, even as the man grabs me by the throat and presses me against the wall, saying, "Turn it off bitch, or I'll kill you now."

Nims is still not moving. Everything hurts, and I hear a voice in the distance saying, "I said turn it off, bitch!"

I focus on what is in front of me. I have to reach her. My hands are beating against the man that has me by the throat, and there are flames sprouting from my skin. Oh fuck, what is happening? The man slams me against the wall again.

I can't hear what he is saying over the flames.

CALLUM

I hear Olivia scream in pain just as I see Nims hit the wall. Oh fuck, fuck, fuck. I quit trying to avoid killing my father's goons and make quick work of them. The two of them dissipate into dust as I end their long lives. I turn to see Olivia covered in flames.

Dammit.

This is what Blair was talking about. The man holding her slams her against the wall, shouting at her. Her eyes become flames. That is my cue. I look down the alley, and I see a door. Racing against her explosion, I can feel the tiny space heating as I scoop Nims up. With her safely in my arms, I sprint for the door and snatch it open. It slams shut behind me, and the explosion rocks the building. Nims is still healing, so I bite into my own wrist and hold it over her mouth. It isn't long before she laps at the blood. When she appears to be fully healed, I quit holding my wrist open and ease her down to stand on her own. She whimpers as she tries to stabilize her feet under her. Looking her over, I see one of her legs isn't right. I ease her down to lie on her side. "Your leg isn't set right to heal. I can put it back in place but, it's going to hurt. I need to get you back to Olivia. If I put your leg back in place, can you keep from attacking me?"

The dog nods and looks away.

"All right." I get my hands positioned on her leg. "Here we go. One, two, three!" I snatch her foot away from the rest of her leg and slowly guide it back into what I feel fairly certain is the place it belongs. She howls as I work, but doesn't struggle or fight me. When I have finished, her howls subside. I wait long seconds to see if it worked, though I am desperate to get back to Olivia.

After a bit, Nims works to heave herself up off the floor. She whimpers a little when she first puts weight on the foot but is quickly able to stand normally. Once she is good, I touch the door. It feels warm but not hot and doesn't seem to do damage to my hand. "Careful out there. Things may still be on fire."

The dog huffs at me like she wants me to get on with it already. Opening the door, we can hear Olivia crying, sobbing her heart out. Nims shoves past me to bolt out the door. I follow her more carefully as she runs to Olivia and covers her in licks. Olivia realizes that Nims is there and alive, and her tears intensify as she throws her arms around the dog. "I thought you were gone! How? Are you all right?" Nims nudges her face and steps back a little to look at me. Olivia follows her gaze and says, "You? Did you save Nims?"

"Yeah. I did. So, um, Blair kind of told us this was coming. We are supposed to take you to see Ailsa—" I cut off what I was saying as Blair and Duncan run into the alley. "Ah, the cavalry has arrived."

People are peering down the alley as they walk by. Blair and Duncan stand next to Olivia and Nims. They are asking all the usual questions, forgetting that we need to get her away from here and over to see the witches.

After giving them a few minutes, I step over and tell them, "Olivia is fine, and so is Nims. Perhaps, we should go to the witches? Unless that plan has changed?"

Blair nods, "You're right. I wasn't thinking. Come on, let's get you up and over to see Ailsa. She'll be waiting for you with how loud that was."

Olivia stands but asks, "Why do I need to see Ailsa?"

Blair stares at her for a beat. "So you can learn how to control that. I know you would hate to harm anyone you didn't intend to. That means you need some training. Don't worry, the witches aren't like the vampires. They don't need to control you to train you. Ok?"

She takes a shaky breath and nods, her hand on Nims head. I tell them I'll catch up as they leave the alley. Going back to find the dust that is the vampires that were attacking us and sifting through it, I find wallets and rings to look at later. I have a feeling I know where they came from, but I need to check first.

Chapter Twenty-Six

It's been two weeks since I combusted. Two weeks of daily meetings with Ailsa, and some witches hating me a little for the personal attention I am getting. Two weeks of Duncan fussing over me like I gained a new power and suddenly couldn't operate my daily life. Blair and Callum have been amazing. Not at all making me feel closed in.

All I want to do is go back to the place I grew up and ask my parents some questions. Ailsa doesn't know exactly what I am. She does know that I am not what they intended to create. When I asked her what they intended, she told me I was supposed to be a sacrifice. Makes me feel super warm and fuzzy toward my parents. Maybe I should go bite them.

Still, I wonder if she's right. Did they work to have a child solely for the purpose of sacrificing her? Is that why the church is still after me? Is it because they planned to sacrifice me? To who? I thought god wasn't dealing in human sacrifice anymore. I thought that was who we were praying to in church.

Getting my phone out, I pull up my mother's social

media. She is still posting missing flyers of me. But with recent pictures? What the fuck? Last seen in Italy? How does she know I was there? She knows I came back to Inverness. Oh, my god. Was the church behind the attack?

Springing up off the couch, I run to find Callum with Nims behind me. He was the only one that saw their faces with me. I find him in his bedroom, laying on the bed and staring at the ceiling. "Callum, I'm sorry to bother you."

He sits up and says, "You are never a bother. Come in, sit."

He crosses his legs on the bed, so there is space. Nims leaps onto the bed and rests her head on his leg. "I guess she is getting used to you."

Callum scratches behind her ear as I settle on the opposite end of the bed. "She probably likes me a little better because I set her leg after I got her out of your line of fire."

"Maybe. I have a question about that day. Do you know who sent those vampires?"

He focuses on scratching Nims head. "They were technically part of the family. But they are part of Diane's line, not my father's. I hadn't mentioned it to you prior because it never seemed like the time. But there is something else you should know. Diane was working with the religious organization that is after you. They were planning to pick you up in Italy."

"What? Why didn't you tell me this before?"

"To be really honest, I didn't want to be the one to make you sad again."

"Dammit, Callum, I can live with being sad. These people want me dead. Sacrificed to something. These people are dangerous. They almost won the last time they attacked. I didn't know they knew I was in Italy, or that I had come back here until I searched for my mother's social media. It isn't safe for me to walk in Inverness. And apparently, the vampires aren't necessarily safe either. Fuck." I nibble on a fingernail, trying to decide what I should do. When I realize what I have to do first, I tap my phone to pull up Roman's number. Tapping the call icon and putting it on speaker because I don't enjoy holding the phone to my ear, and it isn't like Callum isn't going to hear the whole conversation, anyway. Roman answers, and I launch straight into everything. I tell him about my mother's social media, the attack, who exactly it was that attacked us, and that they know I have returned. At the end of my speech, I remember to tell him that he is on speaker and Callum is with me.

He says, "I'm sending Duncan and Niall in a car. All of you, including the wolf, if he is there, come to my house. Callum, you too. Pack a bag. You'll be here for a while."

We end the call and Callum says, "Well, this is going to be interesting."

Rhiannon Futch is a paranormal romance author and Chaos Coordinator, tarot deck collector, rescue dog mom, and craft enthusiast. She has been published since 2019 and is happily settled into writing vampire smut.

Record screech noise here Until the 2024 election she was happily settled into the one genre. Now she is also writing feminist horror novellas, blending her feminism with a dark nature and an immense well of feminine rage.

Wolfie, She-ra, and Daemon are her fully spoiled doggos who live for outdoor games and treat time. She is a night owl with a deep love of fall and winter and teaches yoga to authors but has never managed a headstand.

She is rarely found out in the world, preferring deep woods in the winter and cool writing spaces during the summer. Rhiannon lives in eastern North Carolina currently, with hopes of returning to the mountains of western North Carolina.

If you would like to see what books are next or sign up for her newsletter, visit rhiannonfutchauthor.com (You get a free book when you sign up!) You can also use the QR code (on the next page) to get to my website.

The Daughter of the Moon series-

<u>Selena Rose, Daughter of the Moon Book 1</u>

<u>Thorns of the Rose, Daughter of the Moon Book 2</u>

<u>Heart of the Rose, Daughter of the Moon Book 3</u>

The Fate's Chronicles series

<u>A Vampire's Fate</u>

<u>A Vampire's Treasure</u>

<u>A Vampire's Dream</u>

<u>A Vampire's Chase</u>

<u>A Vampire's Fight</u>

<u>Fated for Halloween -</u> only available via email signup

The Belancore Witches of North Carolina series

<u>Witchy Ever After</u>

<u>A Witchy New Year</u>

<u>My Witchy Valentine</u>

Sin series

<u>Sin on a Dark Knight</u>

<u>Sin on a Broken Heart</u>

<u>Sin on a Burning Heart</u>

Sin on a Vengeful Heart

The Vampire Kings Series

Mercy of the Vampire King

Shame of the Vampire King

Pursuit of the Vampire King

Prey of the Vampire King

Reign of the Vampire King

Love and Vampires Series

Olivia's Fall

Olivia's Flight

Olivia's Family

Warriors of the Old Gods series

A Dream of Blood

A Dream of Wolves

A Dream of Stone

A Dream of Ravens

A Dream of Bones

Her Violent Silence novella series

Wolf Goddess

Coyote Offerings

Old Wolf Woman

Witches Reclaimed series

Titles TBD